AN ENGLISHMAN IN PRATTSVILLE

An Englishman in Prattsville

A NOVEL

GARY MACKNIGHT

An Englishman in Prattsville

First Edition.
eBook ISBN: 978-1-7375027-1-5
Paperback ISBN: 978-1-7375027-0-8
Hardcover ISBN: 978-1-7375027-2-2
Library of Congress Control Number: 2021913400

Cover design and art by Gary Macknight
All rights owned by Gary Macknight
Edited by Lynne Cannon Menges

10 9 8 7 6 5 4 3 2 1

Raven Scott Publications: For any questions about usage, please contact: ravenscottpub@gmail.com

This book is dedicated to:

Christine...
Sitting in front of a fire,
gazing out upon the meadow,
with stars over head,
I turn and ask,
what if...

"NOW THIS IS THE LAW OF THE JUNGLE,

AS OLD AND AS TRUE AS THE SKY,

AND THE WOLF THAT SHALL KEEP IT MAY PROSPER,

BUT THE WOLF THAT SHALL BREAK IT MUST DIE."

— *Rudyard Kipling*

Prologue

Thirteen Years Ago

Louis placed one hand palm up on the mahogany desk. He held the knife in the other, resting the blade on his wrist. He leaned into it causing the cold steel to bite into his flesh.

"Do it, Louis," the familiar voice urged him.

Louis bit his upper lip and took a deep breath, convinced this was his only course of action.

The room erupted with the sound of a telephone's ring and Louis jumped, cutting the outer edge of his skin. It was barely a scratch, but deep enough that blood seeped from the wound. He contemplated not answering it.

What difference would one more phone call make?

He hit the speaker button. "Hello?"

"Mr. Kessler, Kathy Cadelli, from Mountain Realty. They accepted your offer, Mr. Kessler. A hundred and twenty acres and the hunting lodge, just what you were looking for. I'll send the papers over right away. Congratulations, Mr. Kessler, you'll soon own a little piece of Prattsville."

Chapter 1
A Quaint Little Town

Prattsville. *It's a quaint little town.* That's what Louis Kessler likes about it, he thinks as he pulls off the interstate. It would be another forty-five minutes driving through the towering green, picturesque mountains of the Catskills before he reaches his destination. Far from the city where he would often remark, *"There are more people on one city block than all five of the surrounding towns,"* Louis feels his stress shed from him like the winter snowfall on a rusty tin roof melting away in early springtime sun. Town after town speeds by, never changing, never growing old. Louis scarcely notices the wooden buildings and dust-paved gasoline stations as he slows to the required limit of thirty miles per hour in the little towns, before applying a slight bit of pressure upon the accelerator, coaxing the Land Rover back to a cruising speed of sixty. Whether for enjoyment or out of necessity, acquiring the 120-acre property was the best thing he has ever done. Between the sale of the estate in England — a not-so-small sheep farm — and Louis's uncanny ability to make money in the stock market, the price had been a minor setback he's never regretted.

He takes his foot off the pedal a hundred yards before entering the small town of Prattsville quietly cruising in just under twenty miles per hour. By the time he reaches the center of town, he's barely creeping, never having to once tap his brakes as he makes the turn into Jim's Great American's parking lot. You can't quite call it a supermarket, even though it has everything this town could ask for. All six aisles would fit nicely in the checkout line of his big box store back home. But that's what Louis loves about it.

Louis has an air about him. If you've never heard him talk, you might think he comes from Park Avenue royalty. But with the delivery of one syllable, his English upbringing cannot be masked. He is British through and through. Truly proper in the way he dresses, in the way he speaks, even the way he walks. But there is something off about his demeanor. Like a convict who's spent too many years in a cell. Longing for companionship, but standoffish.

Everyone knows *of* him, but maybe not *about* him, which he is quite content with. To the locals, he is the Brit who rides into town once, maybe twice a month, picks up just enough provisions to last three or four days, before heading across the parking lot for one last essential element to help him make it through the weekend.

The Catskill Mountain Liquor store was a recent addition, added shortly after Hurricane Irene swept away most of the town. It is a much-needed refuge in Louis's mind.

The crisp mountain air fills his lungs as he exits the truck. The long, hot days of summer have passed, and now the icy, cold fingers of winter are eager to return. It is noticeably cooler, at least twenty degrees below the place he left four hours ago. *May need to light the fire tonight.* He makes his way through the store, gathering milk, eggs, butter, and orange juice. A pound of cold cuts, or "deli meat," as the locals correct him every time, reminding him he's a flatlander no matter how many years he's been coming up to this haven.

Definitely will be needing a fire tonight. He pulls his coat collar up around his neck.

"Winter's coming early," an old man passing by remarks.

"I should say so," Louis responds.

Reason 342 why he loves upstate. People are just friendlier.

It's a town where mud-covered pickup trucks and rusted cars fill the parking lot as the locals stop to cash their paychecks and fill their shopping carts with the weekend supply of Coors Light. A group of men, clad in camouflage vests and bright red baseball caps, hover outside the hardware store. The barbershop of rural America. Louis feels their eyes upon him as he walks to the truck. No doubt the next subject on the agenda of the *"What's his fucking story"* club.

Reason 27 why he hates upstate. If you weren't born here, it's tremendously hard to fit in.

With the groceries comfortably nestled in the truck, he makes his way to his second stop. High-pitch tinny chimes announce his arrival as he steps through the door, breathing deep the musky, oak-aged barrel aroma of the shop.

"Morning, Mr. Kessler," the salesgirl says, flashing him a smile as her only other customer concludes his business and heads to the door.

"Morning, Jenny, how's your mum?" He holds the door open for the weekend tippler before starting down the aisle.

Jenny breathes deeply, drinking in the words pouring from Louis's lips like fine brandy her customers seldom purchased.

"Oh! I got your bottle all wrapped up for you, and Mom is fine, thanks. A little touch of arthritis. Happens like clockwork around this time of year." Jenny has a wholesome, Donna Reed, *It's a Wonderful Life* kind of look. That's not to say she's plain; she's a natural beauty in the way a summer sunset captures one's attention, makes them stop to drink in the moment before it's lost and gives way to twilight.

"How did you know I was coming today, Jenny?"

"It's been almost 30 days since your last visit. You were due."

"Twenty-six," corrects Louis, and changes the subject quickly. "Yeah, I'm always surprised how people seem shocked that winter comes around every year right after fall."

"When are you going to take the leap and move up here for good?"

"Couple more years, Jenny, a couple more. Just have a few more things to straighten out." He places a hundred-dollar bill on the counter. "As usual, keep the change."

"Mr. Kessler, how many times have I told you, it's way too much—"

He cuts her off. "And how many times have I told you to call me Louis?"

His Fab Four tonality makes her smile girlishly and she buries her chin against her chest. "Thank you, Louis."

He waves the bottle overhead behind him as he makes his way toward the door. "No, thank you. Cheers, Jenny."

Through the store's window, nearly covered with town fliers and illuminated with a red neon OPEN sign, her gaze follows him as he saunters through the parking lot. Like some ancient predator stalking an unaware prey, she remains motionless, eyes fixed. As he slips into the driver's seat, she blinks and is released from her trance. She licks her lips and clears her throat.

Chapter 2
Welcome Home, Mr. Kessler

Louis turns onto the private dirt road. He rolls down his window and punches a series of numbers onto a keypad. A metallic bolt slides. A red circular light on a fencepost turns green, and the galvanized cattle crossing fence swings open, the first hi-tech device within miles of the otherwise rural backwood country. He inches the Land Rover forward at an unusually slow speed clearing the gate before the aggressive tires bite into loose gravel. Behind him, the gate swings back into its home and locks with a clank. The glowing green light switches back to red. Security is restored.

Small valleys and crevasses, cut from the heavy rains, erode the one-lane road that climbs steadily up the side of his mountain. Maneuvering several switchbacks before the road levels out, he applies a little more pressure, coaxing the Rover faster along the dirt road.

Finally, through a tunnel of trees, the cozy cabin comes into view. It's a modest dwelling, nothing like the hardware store boys may have guessed. No log cabin mansion with ten rooms and a jacuzzi on the deck for this transplanted Englishman: a small, one-bedroom, living room, and kitchen, with a dining table able to accommodate no more than four people comfortably, is all he needs.

He puts the groceries away and, before heading outside, checks the second hi-tech device within miles. A state-of-the-art security system assures Louis that the ten-foot-high electronic fence, which runs the perimeter of all one hundred and twenty acres, is live and activated.

The cool night air welcomes Louis as the heavy door closes behind him. Tonight's dinner, a bottle of twelve-year-old scotch, swings in his right hand while the heat from his palm warms the ice-filled glass he carries in his other hand. He sets down the bottle and glass in its customary place on a small table next to a worn-in Adirondack chair. A bright spark from a striking match lights his face before being tossed into a large stone firepit. A pre-made pyramid of dried pine blazes, like a sacrificial funeral pyre. The flames lap at the tiny twigs before spreading to larger logs. With his back toward the pit, Louis watches his shadow rise like a ghastly spectre being summoned from Hell. As Louis pours his first jigger, the flames dance high into the twilight.

He molds to the comfortable chair and brings the glass to his lips, then stops, taking in the smoky oak aroma. The rich caramel color of the liquor appears to change from deep burnt umber hues to bright goldenrod yellows in the fire's light. His lips part and he welcomes the strong, burning elixir into his mouth like a lover's warm kiss. Across the meadow, a deer out for her dusk feeding slowly emerges from the tree line. Louis watches between sips. The timid creature takes a step, looks up, freezes. Moments pass before she takes a few more steps. Cautiously, the graceful doe moves farther into the clearing. Her eyes constantly scan for predators, ears alert and vigilant. A single step. A moment of stillness and a quick graze, before her head snaps upward and she surveys her surroundings. Louis takes another sip. A twig snaps in the forest and she is gone before the whiskey reaches his stomach. Her bright white tail waves in the air, alerting others of her kind there is danger about. Louis thinks, *It's a terrible thing to live in fear.*

Behind him, an old, familiar voice calls out to him. "Hello, Louis."

Louis's body jerks, spilling scotch down the front of him. He moves the glass to his other hand and with a flicker, shakes free the spilt scotch from his arm.

"You would think after all these years you wouldn't get startled."

He takes a generous swig, pouring half the glass down his throat, *Why don't you just leave me alone?*

Chapter 3
The Kill

As twilight turns to dusk, the first speckle of stars pepper the sky. The deep blue sky transitions to a pale orange along the treetops in the west. The trees, now black as ink, stand still and forlorn. Louis is on his fourth glass, the ice long melted. The deep umber spirits slosh from the bottle. Some even make it into the glass. Louis throws the last log of the evening onto the fire, sending sparks of embers dancing high into the night air.

Somewhere, secure on the grounds of the Kessler estate, a stag prepares for nightfall. It's his third time walking the meadow. His keen senses scan his surroundings for any sign of danger. Not a hint of a predator moving through the woods is detected. The stag finds comfort in a secure position where he can oversee the meadow and still retreat safely long before any threat can get within a hundred feet.

A soft yellow glow illuminates the mountain range to the east. The enormous celestial lunar body rises with the last remaining rays of the sun burned upon its face. Blood-red pocked dust will change to a dead yellow hue before coming to rest as the cool gray illuminating glow most people see when they gaze upon the nighttime sky. But on Louis's property, far from any city, where light pollution is almost nonexistent, the moon becomes a surrogate sun. Its rays filter down between the tree branches, lightening the forest floor. Its full strength bathes the meadow in an eerie bluish hue. The air is cool with just a small breeze carrying the scent of the forest through the air. For the stag, it is the best of conditions. A threat can be perceived moving through the meadow, or its scent can be picked up before it ever comes into view. The stag beds down under the pine for the night, secure that it is the safest place to stay until morning. The stag is wrong.

Lying in the tall grass downwind from the pine, a patient predator waits. It has taken the good part of an hour for the beast to obtain his position. With burning yellow-green eyes fixed on the stag, his hindquarters rise ever so slightly, just enough for his back paws to dig their claws into the earth. He raises his front paw, then drops his shoulder as he moves forward and stops, frozen in place. Watching on video, a viewer might think the pause button has been pushed. The beast stays motionless for several minutes before laying the paw back upon the dew-covered grass. Forty-five minutes later and twenty-five feet from the sleeping stag, the stealthy predator crouches low. His hindquarters sway back and forth, set to pounce. Powerful back legs thrust forward. A huge jaw drops, emitting a deep throaty growl.

The stag awakens and takes off. The predator gives chase. It loves the hunt. It prefers it. It is a primal thing. The stag clears fifty yards in four leaps, but its pursuer is closing fast.

The stag zigs and jumps, turns, and runs, but makes one fatal mistake. He heads toward the forest, which is where the predator has the advantage. Moving more quickly than the stag, the beast closes and makes a confident leap, catching the stag's lower back with its claws. Razor-sharp nails dig into the soft hindquarters as the beast's weight drags down the stag. The beast moves quickly, clawing up the back. The stag fights, struggling to get to his feet, trying to run. His efforts are in vain. He knows his fate is sealed. A life lived in fear is coming to an end. Is it possible for the first time, the stag can find peace? A powerful mandible clamps down driving sharp canines into the stag's neck. Blood sprays forth. The beast thrashes his head violently, biting down harder. There's a snap and the stag goes limp. The beast pants heavily, holding the lifeless body in its jaws. Using his powerful legs, he drags the fresh kill deep into the forest. A triumphant howl echoes over the mountains and throughout the valley.

Chapter 4
It's a Hard Knock Life

Not far from Louis's estate, Oren Goodman wakes in the dead of night. Or more appropriately, he has been awakened by a sound not of this earth. He sits up in his bed clutching his covers, waiting to hear the sound again, paralyzed with fear. Oren is a fifth-generation farmer and sleeps in the same room where *his* father died, and his father, and his father before that. He wonders in the darkness if tonight is the night he will die. A ray of moonlight casts the window's portrait across the floor: the only light in an otherwise pitch-black house. His foot slips from the warm blankets and touches the cold, wooden floor.

Oren is used to rising before dawn and has grown accustomed to a hard life. Such is a farmer's life in Upstate New York. The hours are long, and the work is back-breaking. It's far from glamorous, but for Oren, a cold foot on a bare wooden floor in September is of no concern. The thirty-four milking cows are his only concern.

A deep, echoing howl shakes the timbers and seems to be coming from all around. Oren's foot flies back to the bed; his whole body jumps several inches off the mattress. Moments pass and Oren realizes he has not taken a breath since hearing the last wail. He exhales and runs to the door, grabbing his shotgun as he goes.

"Not again," he screams, heading down the stairs. He throws open the front door and enters a world bathed in macabre blue light. He immediately runs to the barn. The cows are huddled in a corner like frightened children.

It must be terrible being the lowest on a food chain, with no natural defenses. And they say sheep are prey for a wolf. At least sheep can run to get away. When was the last time you saw a cow run?

Oren spins around and brings his gun up, sweeping the meadow for any movement, but there's nothing. He fires a warning shot, and then another. The discharge echoes throughout the mountain range. *That should scare off any varmint for miles,* he thinks.

In the distance, the menacing growl replies, proving Oren's theory wrong. When dawn finally creeps over the mountains, basking the green earth with her rays, Oren Goodman is standing in the same spot, with his gun married to his cheek. He's as jumpy as a mother deer. Twitching the shotgun left, then right. His fingers cramp upon the stock and trigger. Even in the cool autumn morning, beads of sweat cover his face. His nightshirt is drenched. He has lived another day. His cows are safe, for now. But his trepidation is real. He fears the beast has returned.

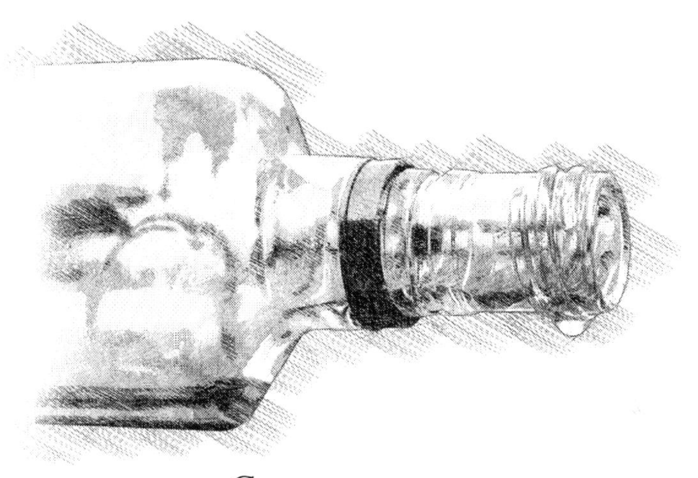

Chapter 5
Hair of the Dog

Louis wakes on a bed of wild grass and dirt, the whiskey bottle lying on its side nearby. The last few ounces of the strong spirit, unable to escape up the neck, remain trapped like a small tidal pool for inebriated insects. He wipes the drool from his cheek and raises his eyebrows, willing his unresponsive eyes to open. Only one heeds the call. The blinding sunlight burns his retina and he quickly wraps his arms around his head in an attempt to block out the morning sun. A chill runs down his back as a soft breeze blows over him. It travels over his skin and shocks his nether region, and he realizes, once again, he has woken up completely naked.

"Every time." He shakes his head. He staggers to his feet. Blinking several times, he tries to get his bearings while allowing as little light as possible to penetrate his brain. His clothes are strewn around the campfire.

"Well, at least I'm close by." He picks up the whiskey bottle and stares at the vestige trapped inside. "I know this isn't your fault, but

I still blame you!" He casts the bottle into the smoldering fire pit. Glass breaks and a fireball erupts like a tiny plane crash, spreading a blanket of blue flame across the tops of the glowing coals.

Louis whips his head around, hearing the distinct sound of tires coming up the dirt road. "Bloody hell!"

He scans the scattering of clothing and thinks, *either retrieve the clothes and get caught naked or make a run for the cabin and come up with a good explanation for the scattered wardrobe.* He chooses the latter and takes off running. Like the central character in Norman Rockwell's painting, *'No Swimming,'* Louis swipes a small article of cloth and modestly covers as much of his manhood as he can. Darting to the bathroom, he lets ice-cold water send shock waves through his body as he rubs his face, neck, and arms vigorously. Incriminating evidence falls into the basin, turning the clean mountain water a reddish-brown. The remnants of last night's escapades wash down the drain as Louis runs to the bedroom and pulls on a pair of jeans. He pulls a T-shirt over his head as the car comes to rest on the patch of lawn designated as the driveway. He barely gets his arms through the sleeves before bony knuckles produce three quick raps on the outside of the screen door.

"You up, Louis?" shouts Jim.

"Sure … sure. Come in. Just putting a kettle on." By "putting on," Louis means flipping a switch on the Mr. Coffee.

"What, did you forget I was coming by?"

"No, no, not at all. It was a rough night," Louis says, running his fingers through his hair and thinking, *I must look like a major wanker.*

Jim looks down at Louis's dirt-covered feet and grimaces.

"It was a really rough night," Louis confesses. "You're lucky you didn't get here ten minutes ago."

"I saw the clothes scattered around the fire pit," Jim says, then asks, "Naked?"

"Naked," Louis answers with a hint of embarrassment in his voice. "Bloody pissed, I was," as if that excuses the fact.

The coffee maker lets loose a concluding *swoosh*, signifying all the water has passed through the ground beans and sits waiting. The aroma of coffee fills the cabin, stronger than in any overpriced Park Avenue trendy coffee shop. Louis grabs two cups from the cupboard.

"I don't know what it is," Louis begins. "Every time I drink I get naked." He hands Jim a cup and sits at the four-person table designated as the dining room. He recalls a story and shares it with his houseguest. "One time, I was in California visiting my cousin and her husband. They took me to this outdoor bar … Mexican, I think. Anyway, we shared five, maybe six pitchers of margaritas."

An inquisitive smirk grows on Jim's face.

"Okay, my cousin and I drank. Her husband was the designated driver."

Jim gives him another doubtful look.

"Okay, okay, I drank maybe five pitchers and my cousin nursed a drink all night." Louis overemphasizes the next word to make his point to move on, "Annnnnyyywaaay, we got back to their house and my cousin turned around and there I stood, in their hallway, wearing a cowboy hat and boots, a poncho and nothing more, whistling, 'The Good, the Bad and the Ugly' soundtrack. Complete with the *Wah, wah, wah*." Louis reenacts the iconic 1966 western theme song by Ennio Morricone.

Jim laughs. "I love that … the song, not the naked part, although that's funny too."

"My cousin still sends me a copy of the movie every Christmas." Louis sips his coffee. "I told that story at a family reunion, and my girlfriend at the time got irritated. When I asked her why, she answered, 'Why do all your stories begin with this one time when I was drunk and naked?' I don't know, I told her. Just something I've always done."

"Boy, remind me never to drink with you." Jim laughs and takes a sip of his coffee.

"You hungry? I can make some bangers and mash?" Louis offers before he corrects for his English upbringing. "I mean, eggs and bacon?"

"No thanks, boss, I'm good. This isn't a social call. I have to check the software." He hesitates. "There is one thing I said I'd pass along to you. Hunting season is coming up and Bobby, Dave, and Joey were wondering …"

Louis knows where this is going; it's the same request every year. Not one of them has ever said as much as a hello to him in town, but come time to nail the prize buck or tear the hell out his property with their oversized ATVs, they're all buddy-buddy. *The pet-shop boys,* Louis calls them, because they remind him of a group of kids hanging out watching the puppies in front of a pet store. Only the pet store is Young's Hardware and Feed.

"Joey is the one with the Humphrey Bogart smile?" Louis asks.

From as early as middle school, Joey Porter had been cursed with oversized *'horse teeth,'* and his classmates had teased him. As Joey's body grew from pubescent youth to manhood, the appearance of his teeth seem to diminished, but his upper teeth still broke through as if he bore a perpetual smile. As a boy, sitting in the dollar movie theater watching *Casablanca* and *African Queen*, Joey begun emulating his Hollywood hero. He would walk around town, pulling his coat collar up, quoting lines from the classic black and white movies.

Jimmy nods.

"And Dave; I'm assuming he's the Alpha male of the pack?"

Again Jimmy nods.

"What's Bobby's story?"

"Bobby Wilcox? He's okay. He's been in Dave's shadow his whole life. I think he'd jump off the Gilboa Dam if Dave asked him to. And not the side filled with water, if you get my meaning."

Louis smirks, taking a sip of coffee.

"They're a good bunch of guys. Just haven't had the best education, that's all."

"The answer is still no," Louis says firmly.

"I'll tell them." Sounding disappointed, Jimmy adds, "It's just … you have some of the finest deer this side of Albany. I wouldn't mind taking a buck one year for myself. Besides, I could use the meat for winter."

Jim is a hometown boy, and for the past ten years he has been caretaker, groundskeeper, maintenance man, and any other synonymous term Louis can think of to justify paying him the salary he does. Not to mention the real reason Louis wants to keep him on retainer: He's the best IT technician in all of upper New York State. Even if Jim doesn't know how good he is, Louis does. When Louis was searching for someone to keep track of the countless miles of fencing surrounding the property, everyone in town offered Jim Denning's name. Right after asking, *"Why the hell do you want to put a fence around your property for?"*

"Good fences make good neighbors," was all Louis would say.

It isn't just about maintaining the fence security; it's making sure, on the days that Louis is up here, that the fence has adequate electrical current flowing through it. Jim designed the monitor system, and Louis has told him plenty of times to patent his system and sell it on the open market. Jim just shakes his head and says, *"I don't know many people who want to surround the forest with an electrified fence, Mr. Kessler."*

Louis studies Jim from across the table. “I tell you what, and you better make sure the pet-shop boys don’t hear about this …” Louis thinks about his next words carefully. “When I’m not up here, you can take a buck come hunting season.” —Louis’s voice turns stern— “and Jim, ONLY when I’m not up here!”

“You got something against guns, Mr. Kessler?”

“No! It’s not like I want to abolish the Second Amendment or anything like that; I just don’t want to get shot! You may hit me instead!”

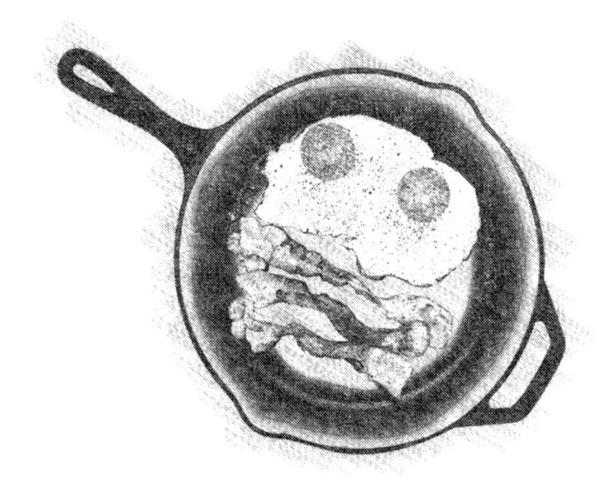

Chapter 6
Getting Noticed In More Ways Than One

Louis gets up from the table, opens the refrigerator, and pulls out bacon, eggs, and butter. "You sure I can't fix you anything? I don't want to get halfway through my breakfast and see you staring at me like some dog begging for scraps."

"No, I had something at the diner this morning," Jim says.

A heavy cast-iron pan heats over the blue flame of the antique stove. Louis peels three slices of thick-cut bacon from the package and lays them across the black surface. "That diner does more business than Sardi's after the opening of a Broadway play." The bacon sizzles. Within seconds, the cabin fills with the unmistakable aroma of pure heaven.

"I don't know anything about that," Jim says, "I never been outside Schoharie County. But Henry sure does fry up a mean over-easy with hash browns."

Louis peels the corner of another slice as the scent teases Jim's nose. "You sure? Now's your last chance?"

Jim waves his hand and graciously declines. "I have to install this new software I've been tinkering with."

Louis turns the bacon and cracks two eggs into the bubbling grease-covered skillet. Translucent yolks instantly turn opaque. "What's this new software do?"

Jim explains in a language way beyond Louis's comprehension. "English Jim, please, in English. Just tell me what it does."

"Oh, I noticed your monthly trips usually occur every 26 to 30 days."

Perturbation grips Louis, freezing him in his spot, with his back turned to Jim. Knuckles turn white. He holds the spatula as if it's a butcher knife in a psycho movie. "Go on."

"So, I got thinking …"

Maybe it's something about the frequency of his visits, or maybe it's something in those four words. A bead of sweat traces down Louis's temple. He focuses on Jim's next few words.

"Why don't I run a program electrifying the fence every 24 or 25 days? It will run for about a week and then shut off. Save you a ton of money."

Louis exhales and drops his shoulders. He covers the pan handle with a dish towel and brings it over to the table where a plate is waiting to receive the banquet.

"What do you think?" Jim asks and quickly adds, "and if you come up unexpectedly, one tap on the space bar and the entire system turns on, easy as pie."

"Sounds like I have a pretty smart IT guy who doesn't know a good breakfast when one's offered to him." Louis laughs before filling his mouth with a heart attack.

Jim sits at the computer and inserts a thumb drive into the USB port. A couple of keystrokes later, Jim watches line after line of code download onto the hard drive.

Minutes later, Louis gets up and places his empty plate in the sink. "Well, I have to run in to town."

Jim fidgets with his hands like a kindergarten student challenging his teacher. "Err, Mr. Kessler … you're gonna shower first, right?"

"YES! Jimmy, I'm *gonna* shower." Louis answers mimicking Jim's upstate accent disguising his English upbringing.

"Oh, good. Because, no offense, but you smell like death."

"Thanks, Jimmy," Louis calls out, heading to, what he would call, the *water closet.*

"Okay, I'll just make sure this is running properly and head out …"

Jimmy's last couple of words barely make it to Louis's ears before the bathroom door shuts. The sound of running water comes from the room, as well as his muffled, "Thanks!"

The sun is high by the time Louis pulls in to the town's main parking lot. The pet-shop boys head straight for Louis, aiming to cut him off before he can enter the liquor store.

"Jim just told us you don't want us hunting on your land!" Dave, the loudest and tactless of the group, shouts as he crosses the parking lot with the other two following like geese in formation. Louis calculates he can make it inside to safe refuge, but he is wrong. The pet-shop boys have him beat by two steps, blocking his path. "Is this true?" the unshaven, unkempt Cro-Magnon barks.

Louis stops, showing no fear, like his mother taught him when bullies picked fights with him on the school playground. "That's right."

Dave is taken aback by the confrontational stand Louis takes.

"Well … well, I want to know why." Dave says, with the others nodding in agreement.

Louis squints. Maybe because of the effects of last night's consumption, maybe because of the audacity of the question. His eyes turn dark and primal, his glare piercing right through his opponent.

"I don't believe I owe you any explanation for why I don't want you on my property," Louis says in a firm, challenging voice. This can only go one of two ways: either Dave and the pet-shop boys are going to creep back to the hardware store, or Louis is going to get his ass kicked in front of Jenny and most of the town.

Louis is expecting the latter, knowing hometown boys just love to fight, and seize any opportunity to do so, but is hoping on the former. To his surprise, even with three against one, Dave shows fear and hesitation. Not committing, but not backing down, either. Having grown up no stranger to being slapped upside of his head, Dave, who easily has thirty pounds over Louis (even though he carries it all in his gut) senses something in the Englishman that puts him off. Still, he takes one more step toward Louis.

Red and blue lights plaster the gang of four and the entire town takes notice as two short, but piercing, *whoa-whoa* blasts come from the siren of a police cruiser.

"This man bothering you, Dave?" the officer yells out the window, leaning across the bench seat.

"No, Pete, we were just talking," Dave yells back. But Officer Peter Hanlon has already slammed the cruiser's gearshift into park. He makes his way around the car. "Why don't you take it back to the hardware store while I have a chat with Mr. Kessler here."

"Sure thing, sheriff." Dave signals to the other two and they head off.

"It's not sheriff. It's officer, Officer Hanlon," he yells at their backs.

Dave mutters under his breath, "I know. It just sounds better."

Louis starts to plead his case but is stopped by an upraised finger as Officer Hanlon watches the trio make their way safely back to Young's Hardware.

"I hope you don't think I thought you were picking a fight with Dave and the boys?" Pete smiles a knowing grin. "Sometimes people have to 'save face,' I believe the Chinese call it? Otherwise, you end up with a bigger mess on your hands. I hope you understand, Mr. Kessler. Dave may be … well, let's just call him dumb, but he has his pride to think about. If I had humiliated him in front of the whole town, I'm afraid he would have had to get even somehow. This way, no one gets hurt … Am I right?" His expression conveys to Louis there is no other response but the one he wants to hear.

"Errr, yeah, sure." Louis tilts his head to the side. "How do you know—?"

"Your name?" Officer Pete interjects. "I make it my business to know the people in this town. And to watch out for them."

Pete Hanlon, though six inches shorter than Louis, stares down the flatlander. His thirty-eight-year-old body may be smaller in height, but is a hundred and ninety-two pounds of solid muscle. In comparison to the salad-eating, marathon-running frame that Louis possesses, Officer Hanlon is a pitbull.

He turns his gaze toward Jenny, who is spying on them both through the store window. He flashes her a smile and tips his hat. More for Louis's consideration, not Jenny's. "Some more than others." His eyes turn toward Louis. "We understand each other?"

Louis nods.

"Good. Then you have a nice day, Mr. Kessler." He tips his hat one more time to Jenny as if to say, *See you later,* and gets back into his car.

Louis walks into the liquor store.

"What was that all about?" Jenny calls to him the moment he steps through the doorway.

"I don't know, what part?" Louis says.

"All of it! What did Dave say to you … What did you say to him? It looked as if you two were going to go at it, right there in the parking lot!"

Louis runs his fingers through his hair.

"OH MY GOD! You're trembling."

It begins with his hands then moves throughout his body. Louis is, in fact, shaking all over. A sudden increase of adrenaline, unnoticeable earlier, now takes hold of his body.

"I haven't been in a fight since prep school."

Fearful his legs will give out, Jenny wraps her arm around him and guides him to a chair. Without thinking, her motherly instincts kick in. "Here, sit down." She kneels in front of him, rubbing his shaking legs. "You should know better than to get into it with those guys."

"I didn't … I mean I didn't want to; he just came at me …"

"So you got up in his face?" She shakes her head. "Men and their egos, I'll never understand it … Me caveman … Me fight!"

"It's not like that. I just came in for a bottle and the next thing I know, I'm about to get my ass kicked and arrested by your boyfriend."

Jenny stands, crossing her arms. "Hold on! My boyfriend?" Is *that* what he told *you*? We're girlfriend and boyfriend?"

Louis opens his mouth.

"If you think I'm dating him … If he thinks I'm dating him! If this town thinks we're dating each other, they should think again! I am no one's girlfriend. Hell, me and him never even went on a date!"

Louis watches as Jenny continues her rant. His shaking has stopped but now he thinks, *out of the frying pan and into the fire.*

"Just because a woman talks to you, doesn't mean she's interested in you!"

Louis shakes his head, afraid to do anything but agree.

"Plenty of men come in here; I'm nice to all of them! It's my job to be nice! I sell more liquor if I'm nice; well, not to the ladies, but I'm nice to them too!"

Louis doesn't know what to do. Sometimes the best course of action is no action.

Towering over Louis, she says, "I'm nice to you all the time … you don't think I like you, do you?"

He shakes his head vigorously.

"You don't, right?"

Shaking is replaced by vigorous nods.

Her face changes with his reaction. "You don't?" Her eyebrows furrow. "Why don't you?"

The nodding slows and bewilderment takes its place.

"I mean, why don't you think I'm interested in you? I stock your favorite whiskey" —she turns to him— "… and you know it wasn't easy to get! Hell, no one drinks twelve-year-old Scotch whiskey … from SCOTLAND up here! Pam sells more Budweiser and Coors in Jim's Great American than Henry sells French toast at the diner." She paces like an attorney desperate to get her client off death row. "I even wrapped the bottle for you yesterday. I mean, who does that?"

Louis stands up.

"Why do you think I did that?"

"To sell whiskey?" he timidly offers.

"No, you jerk, I just wanted you to notice me." Tears well up in her eyes.

"I thought you were just being nice," he says, moving closer.

Her chin drops onto her chest. "I wanted you to notice me. I wait all month for you to come through that door."

Louis awkwardly tries to comfort her.

"You're the best part of my whole day." She throws her arms around his neck and cries. "You're the best thing in this whole stinking town!"

Across the parking lot, Officer Hanlon watches through the window as Louis comforts her. He lets loose two more short bursts from his siren as he exits the parking lot. The whole town freezes, as does Louis who, even through the store window and across the parking lot, catches the death stare thrown his way, right before Officer Hanlon pulls the police cruiser out on Main Street and guns the engine.

Two small fingers gently touch Louis's freshly shaved cheek and guide his attention back to where it should be. "I'm nobody's girlfriend," she whispers. Her soft lips touch his. *I'm going to be the best thing in your life!*

Chapter 7
Interview

"Good. Then you have a nice day, Mr. Kessler." Officer Hanlon tips his hat one more time to Jenny and thinks, *I could make you so happy, Jenny. If you only gave me a chance.*

He walks back to the cruiser, glancing over at Dave and the boys. *One day you're going to pick a fight with the wrong fella and I'm not going to be there to save your ass.* He circles the parking lot, but instead of leaving he parks the cruiser next to the grocery shop and watches as Louis enters the liquor store.

Through the window he sees Jenny usher Louis over to a seat before disappearing in front of him. *What the hell is she doing,* he thinks, and sits up, adjusting his position to get a better view. One inch higher does not afford him that luxury. Thirty seconds more, and he is going in. Nervous fingers drum on the steering wheel.

"That's it!" His hand flies to the door handle and stops just as Jenny bolts upright, hands crossed. He's seen this stance before. It's not good. He smirks, knowing poor old Louis is about to experience Jenny's wrath. *You're boxing outside your league,* he thinks as Jenny unleashes arms of fury waving in all directions. A grin widens on Officer Hanlon's face. He's really enjoying himself. It feels good, for once, not being the person on the receiving end of Jenny's rants.

It's all over, lover boy. She's got you up against the ropes, the voice inside Pete's head proclaims. Louis is shaking his head frantically, then he begins nodding. Pete's inner narrator starts commentating as if he were at a prize fight. *Oh, it's a real bloodfest here tonight, folks. The contender is weaving and bobbing, but it won't do him any good. I've never seen this gal lose yet, I'm predicting a knockout in four, three, two, one.*

He watches as Louis stands. *Keep walking, Jenny one, our contender from across the pond Mr. Kessler, zero!*

BUT wait, sports fans, the announcer in his head cries. *Our contender is moving in closer.* Officer Pete's smile drops.

A crack and then an electronic dispatcher's voice fills the car. "Car four, car four, come in!"

Pete grabs the mic, not taking his eyes off the unexpected scene playing out in front of him. "I'm here, Vilma."

"We got a call from Oren Goodman. To say he's perturbed is an understatement, talking about something is back and it's after his cows again. Over!" The static voice cuts out.

"He saw … WHAAAAAT!" Officer Pete yells into the mic as Jenny throws herself into Louis's arms.

"He wouldn't say, or couldn't say, or maybe I just couldn't understand him on account of him yelling so fast. Better get over there and see what's up … Over."

"Yeah! I'm on it!" he shouts, throwing the mic to the floorboard. The tightly wound coil slingshots it back, and it hits him in the chest before coming to rest at his feet. He grunts and slams the cruiser's gearshift into drive and heads to the exit. He hits the siren two more times as a warning. One last ogle before answering the call of duty. Fuming, his foot collides with the pedal, sending the cruiser screeching up Main Street — an offense that he surely would have issued a ticket for if it wasn't him doing the offending.

Twenty-five minutes from town Officer Hanlon heads down the winding road that leads to Oren Goodwin's farm, visions of Jenny doing unmentionable things in the back room with Mr. Fancy Talker in his head. The beautiful green pastures and rolling hills where Officer Pete has lived his whole life provide little comfort in calming his ever-growing rage. Over and over, the scene of Jenny placing her arms around him burns in his neo-cortex. The closer he gets, the more he turns his anger to Oren.

"This better not be a wild fucking goose chase!" he says, talking to himself as he often does on long drives. He comes over the crest of a hill and there in the distance, cutting through the tree line and lining the left side of the country road, is a menacing ten-foot-high electrical fence. Square, yellow, posted *Private Property Keep Out* signs, along with red *Danger Electrified* warning signs are spaced every twenty feet along the fence. Officer Hanlon feels his blood pressure hit a new high. He raps his palm down heavily on the steering wheel.

"Perfectly good countryside and he goes and shits it all up!" He eyes the fence as he passes, becoming almost mesmerized by the constant breaks in the steel links by towering posts and colorful signs. "I'm starting to really hate this guy."

He turns his eyes back to the road just in time to spot a chicken standing dead center on the asphalt pavement. "GOD! Damn it!"

He slams both feet down on the brake pedal. Metal shavings of copper, steel, graphite, and brass bonded with resin, the cruiser's brake pads bite down into the hot steel, locking the tires, leaving twenty feet of Goodyear Viva 3 All-Season rubber on the road. The nose of the cruiser dips, coming to a full stop before rocking up as the car's weight is once again displaced, and the unruffled poultry strolls to the side of the road.

"Goddamn it." This time his words come out less in excitement and more in disbelief. "Animal's too stupid to know it's someone's dinner."

Officer Hanlon proceeds at a more reasonable speed as he pulls up to Oren Goodman's farm.

Oren, shotgun still in hand, shouts from his front door. "It's back!"

"Damn it, Oren, I almost ran over one of your chickens back there."

"It's back!" Oren shouts again, moving fast from his porch, getting closer to the cruiser. "I'm telling ya' it's back!!!"

"Whoa! Calm down, Oren. And do me a favor and put down the shotgun. Hell, if I didn't know you, you'd be on the ground already with hands cuffed."

Oren, unaware of the gun, doesn't seem to realize at first it could be perceived as an instrument of death. "Oh." He searches for someone to give it to then starts to lay it down on the ground.

"Here, give it here." Pete signals with a wave of his hand.

Oren is reluctant but offers up the gun. "It's out there. I heard it."

"Don't worry, you'll get this back when we're done here," Pete presses the small button by the trigger guard and slides the forestock back and forth several times, ejecting the remaining cartridges. Bending over, collecting the shells, he says, "Now what's this all about? Who's out there? What's back?"

Chapter 8
Confession

Jenny's lips are warm and inviting, soft and tender. Louis closes his eyes and gets lost. Lost in feelings he has not felt in a long time. Feelings buried deep, locked away, hidden from the world. He gets lost wrapped in her arms. Lost in a feeling of comfort and safety. Louis longs for the security one gets from being held by someone who truly loves them. He spends long nights pining to know the pleasures granted to average men. He aches to feel the mundane, trivial, routine life most men take for granted and bitch about at local pubs or taverns. A life he will never know. A life denied at birth. He allows himself this single momentary selfish desire to feel … to feel what it would be like to have the love of a beautiful woman. A woman who earnestly desires him.

Louis presses his lips against hers. She breathes deep, knowing her advances are reciprocated. Her heart beats faster. She becomes flushed and something tells her, *he's the one.*

Louis's eyes open wide, realizing what's happening. Nightmarish thoughts deeply repressed wake from the blackness and devour any thoughts of a normal life Louis could have had. Louis grabs Jenny's arms and pulls away. "Jenny, I'm so sorry … I should have never …"

Jenny's shocked expression hurts more than the ass-kicking the pet-shop boys could have ever inflicted.

"Jenny, I want to …" he begins.

She buries her chin against her chest, this time not in a flirtatious way, but more of an embarrassed, shameful way. "I should have never …"

"No! No, it's my fault, I should have never kissed you …"

Her eyes connect with his. "Louis, I kissed you."

"But I kissed you back … and I wanted to … but it was wrong." He searches for the right words to say. The hurt expression once again returns to her face. "I have a—"

"Oh my God! You have a wife!" she cries and covers her mouth with her hand.

"No! No!" He reaches for her but she pulls away. He raises his hands as if Officer Hanlon has his gun drawn and just caught him running out of the First National Bank with sacks of money. "It's not that. I have a … a … a disease."

Jenny furrows her brow, and then a light goes off and her eyes become sympathetic. She cocks her head to the side. "Oh, Louis, I know you do."

"You do?" Now it's Louis's face that looks puzzled.

"Hell, half the people in this town have that disease. Why do you think this shop does so well? I'm not that good a salesgirl, Louis! Most everyone up here are alcoholics."

"Jenny, I'm not an alcoholic," Louis protests.

Jenny smirks. "Louis, no one buys a bottle of 12-year-old

Macallan, then comes back the next day to buy another one, without being an alcoholic. It's no shame, Louis; half my family drinks till they pass out." She walks over to him and rubs his arm. "We can work through this. If you want help, I can get you help, and if you don't … well, I've lived with worse."

"Jenny, listen to me. That's not the disease I'm talking about."

She pulls her arm back.

"It's not that kind of disease; you can't catch it. No one can, it only affects me." His voice drops, low and somber. "My mother told me I contracted it from my father. Something in his DNA." He sits on the bench. "She didn't know he had it when they slept together. Of course, what do you expect? You're a nurse in a hospital and you bring a patient home with you …" Louis explains as if he's in his therapist's office, then stops abruptly, fearing he's said too much. He glances at his watch. "Shit, I've got to get back." His mind races as he heads to the door and stops. "Can I see you tomorrow? I'll explain everything."

She nods, and he turns to leave. He stops and spins. For a moment she thinks, *He's going to kiss me again,* but Louis's gaze sweeps the shelves.

"I need something …" He grabs a bottle of Schoharie Shine, a man-in-the-moon illustration on the label. "That figures," he leers.

He pulls fifty dollars out for a twenty-seven-dollar bottle and places it on the counter. "Sorry, Jenny, I really am, but I have to go."

She watches him get into his truck and drive away, "Not an alcoholic, my ass!"

Chapter 9
It Stood

It takes Officer Hanlon a good fifteen minutes of listening to Oren babble before he pieces his story together.

"And you think this thing you heard last night is the same animal that mutilated your cows ten years ago?"

"That's exactly what I'm saying, Pete. And it ain't no animal!" Oren starts pacing, "I saw it! Ten years ago! And I don't ever want to see it again!"

"You sure it wasn't a coyote or maybe a large wolf?"

"Does a coyote stand upright on his hindquarters?" Oren asks forcefully.

"Maybe a bear?" Pete offers.

"IT AIN'T NO BEAR! And it ain't no coyote, or wolf, or mountain lion, or any other animal I ever seen!" Oren paces more frantically.

"Okay, okay, calm down and tell me, one more time, exactly what happened ten years ago."

Oren stops dead in his tracks and takes a deep breath. His eyes glaze over, and he begins. "It was the spring, right before that sweltering summer when the upper reservoir stopped flowing."

"It was, like most years, uneventful. One day blurring into the next, one-year blurring into the next. But this year was different. A lot was going on. That new guy, the British guy Kessler, bought up all that property. I didn't care. Nice enough fella. Told me he didn't have a problem with my cattle grazing on what was now his property. Really nice of him." Officer Hanlon catches the sarcasm in Oren's voice and smiles.

"Anyway, like I said, all uneventful until, I believe it was the middle of June. One night the cows got skittish toward nightfall, moving together in a herd, not wandering like they normally do."

"Cows don't travel in herds?" Pete asks.

"They do if there's something stalking them," Oren answers, then continues. "Not many predators out here. Oh, sure, you get your occasional coyote stray or even a pack, but they usually take down rabbits or a small fawn. Maybe even a doe, but taking down a buck is dangerous for them. Too risky and once one of them gets injured, well, let's just say they become another option on the menu. If you get my meaning?"

"I hear yah." Pete nods. "Dog eat dog world, pardon the pun."

"The what?" Oren turns his head.

"Nothing, go on."

"Anyway, it's highly unlikely that coyotes will go after my cows. I mean, I guess it's possible, if they were hungry enough, but I never seen them even try. No sir, not in all my years, and not in my daddy's years either. But something had these cows spooked."

Oren stops and thinks. "Then one night, just like last night, I woke from a dead sleep. Strangest howl I ever heard. It was far off in the distance, but it was unlike anything I heard. I got up and went to the window."

"You didn't really expect to see anything, did you? Must have been pitch black, Oren."

"Not that night. Moon lit up the entire valley. Had an eeriness to it, like out of a Halloween movie."

"So what did you see?"

"Nothing, not a damn thing. But I figured that was the thing scaring my cattle. So, I loaded my gun and waited."

"Waited for ...?"

"Waited for about two months!" Oren chuckled. The first time since Officer Hanlon had arrived here that he'd heard some kind of levity in Oren's voice. Maybe he was just happy Officer Hanlon was not calling him a nutcase and driving back to town.

"Then, again, in the middle of the night, that awful howling came again. Unearthly, I tell you. I grabbed my gun and ran outside. Something was moving in the fields, but I couldn't get a look at it." He bends down and hunches his shoulders. "It was real low, like crawling, maybe stalking like a bobcat would do, but stealthy."

"If you didn't see it, how did you know it was out there?"

"You ever been hunting, Pete?"

Pete nods.

"Then you know. It's the same way that deer knows you're there. Besides, I saw the tall grass in the field being pushed to the side as it crept."

Oren brings his hand to his cheek and extends the other arm, holding a pretend gun. "So I, BAM!" He raises both hands in an arching motion. "I fired a couple of shots into the field and waited."

"Anything?"

"Nothing. The next day I went out there. There was something there, all right! Something BIG! But no sign of blood, fur, or droppings."

"You mean scat?"

"Yeah. Shit."

Pete smirks. "I was trying to use a forensic term. So, you scared it off?"

"Not exactly. For the next couple of nights I would hear it howl. I would go outside and fire off a couple of rounds, and in the morning, not a sign. Then nothing for a long while."

"You mean a couple of days?"

"No, a couple of months. Then fall came, and the son of a bitch got one of my cows! And that pissed me off. Tore the thing all to hell. Its neck was ripped open, stomach and innards spewed twenty feet in every direction. Enormous pieces of meat ripped from bone. I'm telling ya, Pete, it was a bloodbath. Like four or five lions fought over this poor cow."

Pete stops writing. "So you think it was more than one?"

"No, it was only one, I said it looked like four or five fighting over it, but it was only one."

"How can you be sure?"

"Because the next night, I took one of my sickly cows out to the meadow, I tied it to a post …"

"Oh Oren, you didn't."

"I sure did, got up in that old deer stand on the edge of the property back there." He points across the field. "Waited all night. Didn't think the bastard was going to show. Then right around three in the morning when the moon was full, I saw something coming down from the hills. Really cautious like, but it was hungry, and it knew the cow was trapped. It was real big, like a wolf only twice as large. I watched that son of a bitch attack that cow with a vengeance. I got the gun up and just when I was about to pull the trigger, it must have heard something 'cause it stopped and turned. And then it did something I never saw before."

"What?"

"It stood up, turned and looked right at me. I'm telling you, Pete; I almost shit myself! I mean, what kind of animal does that?"

A perplexed Officer Hanlon shakes his head. "And you couldn't make out if it was a bear or wolf or a—"

"It wasn't no BEAR! I told you … Its body was silhouetted against the grass, the fur was a black mass. If it weren't for the moonlight that caught its eyes and jaw, I would have thought it was a man. That's why I hesitated. The thing was already running by the time I got two shots off. It started off on two legs, then dropped down and took off. Shit, Pete! I mean, what kind of animal can do that?"

"None that I know of," Officer Hanlon tries to comprehend what Oren has just told him. "And you're sure …"

"It stood, Pete! As sure as I'm standing right now."

"And you haven't heard or seen it since?"

Oren shakes his head. "Not till last night. I thought maybe I scared it off, but I don't think that thing is scared of anything. Then I got thinking: it was right around the time when that English fella put up that fence."

"The electrical one?"

"I don't think it was electrified when it first went up, but that's the one."

"So you think that thing came from Kessler's place?"

"I'm not saying he brought it up here, but maybe he trapped it on his property when he put the fence around it. Either way, I don't care. I just don't want it getting to my cattle! I can't afford to lose any more heads of cows. Times are tough and only getting tougher."

"I hear ya there, Oren. Okay, don't worry. I'll have a little chat with Mr. Kessler, and if he's stocking his property with dangerous animals, I'll have the state game warden here quicker than you can fire off a round."

He hands Oren back his shotgun. "Oh and hey, if you bag that thing, I'd love to see it mounted at Young's!"

"If I get it in my sights next time, that thing's going on my wall!"

Officer Hanlon smiles as Oren laughs.

"Thanks for coming out, Pete."

"That's what friends do. Take care of those cows, Oren." Pete shakes his hand.

Pete backs the cruiser up and heads down to the county road, now with another reason to have a chat with Louis. *Maybe Mr. Kessler will have concluded his business with Jenny and I'll just pay him a visit.*

CHAPTER 10
A FRIENDLY CHAT

Louis shakes his head. *Stupid, stupid, stupid,* he repeats, tossing the bottle on the passenger seat. He pulls out of the parking lot and heads for the cabin.

"You were going to tell her!" A familiar voice comes from the back seat.

"No I wasn't," Louis protests.

"Yes, you were! What are you, crazy?"

Louis stares in the rearview mirror. "Seriously?"

"Sorry, wrong choice of words, but seriously, Louis, you can't tell her. Do you remember what happened the last time you even hinted at your situation?"

Louis nods.

"Yeah, you almost spent a month in the psych ward. If it weren't for me getting you out in time, you would have—"

"I know what I would have done."

"You want to go through that again?"

"No, but I care for her. She's not like …" Louis can't bring himself to say her name.

"Nicole!" the voice admonishes. "Do I need to remind you what happened to her?

Louis is quiet.

"Do you want me to *show* you what happened to Nicole?"

"Goddamn it, WHY don't you leave me alone?"

Louis reaches for the bottle. Taking a turn a little too fast, he corrects his steering and manages to get the top off on a straightaway. The cold glass rim touches his lips and he quickly downs a quarter of the bottle before tearing it way from his mouth. He resists his body's urge to vomit up the offensive liquid. He brings the bottle up again and sees Officer Hanlon's distinct blue and yellow cruiser speed by. In his rearview mirror, the car makes a U-turn and its blue and red lights flash in repetition. "Shit!"

Louis pulls over to the shoulder. The cruiser pulls up behind him. He sits drumming his fingers, waiting for the customary two minutes to go by before Officer Hanlon exits his patrol car, adjusts his hat, and makes his way up to Louis's driver's side window.

"Was I speeding, Officer?"

"Mr. Kessler, just the person I wanted to talk to." Hanlon takes a quick glance at the truck's interior. "And let's cut the bullshit about 'Was I doing anything wrong, Officer?'"

"Let me just say, nothing happened with me and Jenny."

"We'll get to that later, but right now, would you mind stepping out of the truck?"

Adrenaline keeps the effects of the moonshine, already absorbed into his bloodstream and racing toward his brain, at bay as Louis exits his truck. He twists his wrist, and a glance at his Rolex Daytona reminds him *not much time left.* "Did I do something wrong?"

"Just a few questions, Mr. Kessler, then you'll be on your way." Officer Hanlon spots the moonshine on the seat.

Louis smiles sheepishly.

"I was just at the Goodman farm." Officer Hanlon notices that Louis bends his head. "Oren Goodman. He has the dairy farm that butts up to the back of your property."

"Oh, yeah."

"I believe you can see the old Kearney cabin from the road? Well, when the view's not being obstructed by that fence of yours."

Louis opens his mouth but Officer Hanlon just keeps talking. "Boy, that sure is some fence you got there. Does it go all around your property?" already knowing the answer.

Louis nods, "Yes, yes it does."

"And why would you suppose someone needs a fence like that? Who you trying to keep out?"

"It's not *who* am I trying to keep out, sir. It's *what* I'm trying to keep in."

Officer Hanlon gets real serious. "And just what is it you're trying to keep in? Anything big enough to take down a cow?"

"A cow? No, I don't think so." Louis feels his right eyebrow droop and compensates for it by taking a deep breath and exhaling.

"Then why the fence, Mr. Kessler?"

Louis prays he doesn't slur any words. "After I purchased the property, a friend sold me a dozen Scottish red deer. They're much larger than American deer and truly beautiful. Expensive, I might add. So you see, I couldn't have them running off all over the Catskills."

"Are you a hunter, Mr. Kessler?"

"If you're asking if I've stocked my property with deer so I can come up here whenever I want and feel the thrill of the hunt, the answer is no. They're majestic beasts and don't deserve to be gunned down from a tree stand hundreds of yards away while they take a sip of water from a babbling brook. I certainly don't want to see any of their heads mounted on someone's trailer park wall. No sir, that's not my idea of hunting."

"But you do hunt?" Pete presses.

"I've killed my share of game, but only when the law allows, and never for sport." He catches Pete's gaze, staring him dead in the eyes. "I eat what I kill."

Officer Hanlon sees something more than the timid city slicker who almost got his ass kicked. He moves on with his line of questioning. "You have any bears on your property?"

"I may have a black bear. That might be who wanders around eating from my pear trees in the summer, but I can't be sure."

"Any coyotes or big cats?"

Louis's cell phone alarm goes off, "Do you mind if I …" He gestures toward the truck. "Otherwise it will keep buzzing till I shut it off."

Officer Hanlon nods, and Louis retrieves the phone to silence the alarm. "What's this about, if you don't mind me asking? Are you taking a survey of wild animals in the general area, or just mine?"

"I got a call from Oren Goodman, seems something was stalking his cows the other night. I was just wondering if maybe something could have gotten off your grounds."

Louis shakes his head. "No, I don't see how anything might have. The fence is mainly to protect the Red Deer from wandering off. Do you think my deer are in danger?"

"Have you noticed any missing?" Officer Hanlon asks.

"I don't count them every time I'm up here, so it's hard to tell."

"Have you heard any strange noises at night?"

"Strange noises? No, I wouldn't say strange, but those Scottish Deer have a unique mating call. Perhaps that's what he heard?"

"Oren said it sounded like growling or howling."

"Growling? No, nothing like that. I'm usually outside by the fire at night, and I can't say I've heard anything strange. Actually peaceful; that's why I come up here, to get away. Did he say what it was?"

"He couldn't say. Hell, I don't even think it was anywhere near him, from how he tells it. It could have been by the old Kearney place. That's why I'm asking … You got anything big on your property that likes to eat cows?"

Louis nervously laughs. "Just me, with some fried onions and peppers."

Officer Pete is not amused.

"Look, Officer Hanlon, I'm heading home tomorrow, but if you want, I'll have Jim Denning give you the security code. You can search the property to your heart's content." Louis's attention returns to his watch. "And you have my permission to remove any animals that you find threatening to Mr. Goodman's cows."

"That's the second time you looked at your watch. You got somewhere to be, Mr. Kessler?"

"Is this going to take much longer? The market is opening up in Japan. That's kind of how I make my money." Louis is only partially lying.

"Just what is it you do for a living?" Officer Pete asks.

"Right now, I'm losing money." Louis feels a thin sheen of perspiration build on his forehead. "Can we continue this discussion in the morning, Officer? I'll be happy to answer all your questions tomorrow, but right now I need to get home."

"Just a few more, Mr. Kessler," Officer Hanlon, annoyed by the way Louis has dodged his question, thinks, *I don't care how much money you lose. We'll sit here all night if we have to.* "Are you married, Mr. Kessler?"

"Am I what?"

"Married? Have a girlfriend? Maybe living with someone in the big city? Maybe have to tell her, or them" —he makes the ambiguous innuendo and continues— "that you need to get away for a weekend on business or visit an old friend, and you come up here and start hitting on the locals?"

"I bought this place to be alone! Oh, I see what this is about. Listen, Jenny and I are—"

"Is that alcohol I smell on your breath, Mr. Kessler?"

Louis throws his hands up. "You got me. I took a sip to calm my nerves after almost getting the shit kicked out of me by your fine upstanding townsfolk—"

"Driving while impaired is still an offense in Schoharie County, Mr. Kessler, so unless you want to spend a night in jail, I'd take that language down a notch."

"I'm just saying, half the folks leaving the tavern on a Friday night have way more alcohol in their bloodstream than I do. I'd bet by the time we got back to town, I wouldn't even blow a .01."

"You really want to make that bet?" Officer Hanlon threatens.

Sheepishly, Louis answers. "No, not really. I just want to get home and start working."

Officer Hanlon looks at him for a long time, trying to decide if this is a battle he wants to continue fighting. Here's a guy who's already almost been in a fight, now getting harassed by local police for taking a sip of alcohol, and all he wants to do is get home. Even that thing with Jenny could be a misunderstanding, Jenny was just being nice. Then he comes to the conclusion that this Brit, when it comes down to it, really has done nothing wrong. He concedes it's best for another time.

"Okay then. Well, since you've been so upright in answering all my questions, I guess we can let this first offense slide." Officer Hanlon opens Louis's door for him.

Louis gets in his car.

Still watching him like a hawk, Hanlon says, "You have a good night Mr. Kessler, And keep a cork in that bottle till you get home."

"Will do, officer." And then Louis eats some crow, adding, "and thank you."

Pete smiles and thinks, *We're going to get along fine, as long as you know who's top dog in this town.*

Louis doesn't start the Rover until Officer Hanlon turns his cruiser around and heads back to town. He starts the engine, grabs the bottle and uncorks it. Downing half of the remaining contents, he hears from the back seat, "FLOOR IT, LOUIS, DRIVE! DRIVE!!!"

He slams his foot down on the accelerator. Tires spin, a cloud of dust fills the air, and the smell of burnt rubber wafts into the cab of the truck as the rear end fishtails. Louis prays he is not too late. His phone alarm goes off again. "Shit!" he yells, bringing the bottle of spirits to his lips for the second time.

By the time he reaches the gate, the bottle is empty, and the moonshine has effectively done its job. A hazy cloud blurs Louis's vision. The Land Rover sways from side to side on the country road. The sun has set and its fleeting light barely pierces the shadows, making the forest cover seem even darker. Louis inches his truck closer to the gate, trying to find the entrance keypad in the dark.

His hand falls to the console, hitting as many buttons as his fingers can press. Windows all around the truck roll down, flooding the cab of the truck with crisp mountain air. It slaps a small amount of inebriation from Louis's brain, allowing him just enough clarity to focus on the keypad. Fingers stretch forward and miss their mark. Error message after error message flash across the keypad's readout screen, denying Louis entrance. He repeatedly attempts to enter the correct sequence of numbers, to no avail.

"Shhhhhit!" Louis mutters. The bottle of moonshine tumbles from the cab along with Louis, who barely catches himself, locking his arm around the window frame. "Moddthurr Fuddkkkker!" he cries out.

Slamming the door, he staggers, trying to focus on the keypad. Several more failed attempts only infuriate Louis more as a voice calls out, "Hurry Louis, hurry!"

"I'm trrrrying!" Louis screams back, looking at the fence like it's an impenetrable foe. And then an idea invades his thoughts. Louis staggers to the fence.

What if ... He stands contemplating. *It will only hurt for a second, then all this will be over.*

"Do it! Louis," a voice whispers in his ear.

He raises his palms, swaying, trying to steady himself. *Don't wimp out, Louis.* He takes a deep breath. His last breath on earth. He tries to think of any reason not to go through with it ... Nothing comes to grant him a reprieve.

He closes his eyes and thrust his hands forward. Even before his hands clutch the cold steel, he lets out a godawful scream. His fingers lock around the links and his whole body shakes. His legs go limp. Louis's screams of terror slowly die out, like a fire siren after a long steady blast winding down.

No electricity courses through Louis's body. No heart-stopping volts end his life. No execution for Louis Kessler this night.

"What the Fuuuuuckkk!" Louis screams, looking up, noticing the glowing green circular light. "I'mmmm gonnna khilll Jimmmmy," Louis slurs.

"You're out of time, Louis," the voice whispers.

"Fuuuck." He bends his knee, trying to pull his shoe off, then tumbles and falls to the ground. A string of obscenities ramble from his mouth as he pulls his dirt-covered shirt from his body and throws it into the truck. In one fluid motion, he pulls free his belt, kicks his pants free, and stumbles off into the meadow across the road. The dew-covered grass chills his feet. As the bright light of the moon crests over the hills, Louis runs.

Chapter 11
Late Night Call

The Prattsville sheriff's office is small, like most small-town municipal buildings, and sits directly across the street from Jenny's liquor store. In fact, driving through town, most people never even see it, because they're too busy looking at the grocery store on the right. But it's where Officer Hanlon has started and finished every typical twelve-hour day for the past six years. He starts before the sun rises and finishes long after sunset. Tonight is no exception. At quarter to seven, Officer Hanlon is in the doorway, and only Officer Vilma Ortiz is there to man the phones.

"You don't have to come back here to sign out, Peter. We all know how hard you work; no one would say anything if you just head home after your shift," Vilma says.

"Just have to check on one more thing, then maybe I'll go over to the tavern for a burger."

"You should try their pizza. It's amazing." She puts a finger up as her other hand hits the switchboard. "Prattsville Sheriff

Department, how can we help?"

Pete walks to his desk and throws his hat upon the empty chair. He taps the keyboard and the blue-green monitor wakes up.

He types … 'Louis Kessler. New York City.'

With a couple more keystrokes to narrowing his search, and moments later, an assortment of windows enlarge upon the screen, overlapping until they fill the monitor with details about Louis Kessler's entire life. Forgetting the burger, Pete hunkers down for a night of research and enlightenment.

○❩❩❩●❨❨❨○

"Pete! Pete! Wake up!" Vilma yells from the switch board, Peeeeetttee!"

Pete stirs and wipes his eyes, "What time is it?"

"Pete!!!!"

"I'm up, I'm up! What's all the yelling about?" Pete looks at the computer screen. He must have fallen asleep just as he got to the last five years of Louis Kessler's life. His eyes squint at the time clock in the corner of the screen, "Two-fifteen! Vilma! It's a quarter past two in the morning!"

Pete stumbles over to the switchboard where she's trying to get Oren Goodman back on the phone. "Oren! Oren?" Vilma yells.

Pete hears the name and snaps to full attention as Vilma covers the headset's microphone and hits a couple of buttons. She motions to the speaker and both listen to a recorded playback.

"Prattsville Sheriff's Department. How can we—" "It's here!" Oren Goodman's voice cuts off Vilma's. *"Pete, get your ass over here! Now!!!!"*

Something terrifying in his voice sends a chill down both Vilma's and Pete's spines.

"That came in at 2:13 a.m. It's all Oren said. That's when I yelled to you! but wait," Vilma holds up a finger. Seconds later, a shot rings out, then another and another, followed by a scream.

Pete grabs his coat and keys. "This just happened?" Pete says, running toward the door. "Like right now!" Vilma shakes her head, tears welling up in her eyes as she calls into the headset. "Mr. Goodman, Oren, are you there?"

"Keep trying him, tell him I'm on my way."

"Oh, God! Pete, there's growling and screaming like he's being ripped apart by dogs!"

Red and blue flashing lights set Main Street ablaze as Pete's cruiser flies up County Road Seven, Prattsville Road, and disappears into the dark.

Chapter 12
Oren Goodman's Final Day

Twenty-two minutes. It takes twenty-two minutes for Officer Hanlon to reach the doorstep of Oren Goodman's house from the Prattsville police station. Seventeen minutes if he redlines the cruiser, but he runs the risk of losing control and rolling it into a ditch. Either way, Officer Hanlon will not make it in time. The cruiser screams in excess of a 87 miles per hour on the straights before Pete has to apply the brakes. He slows the cruiser to half its speed only to slide into the curves, then pins the accelerator against the floorboard once again. Even at this rate, he will reach the Goodman farm in sixteen minutes. Twenty-five minutes too late. Thirty-six minutes since Orin Goodman woke in terror.

Oren Goodman went to bed at seven-forty, but anxiety and fear kept sleep from coming till exhaustion took hold, and Oren's eyes finally closed around eleven-twenty. Somewhere in the meadow, by the light of the celestial moon, death moved quietly across the field. A single porch light called to him like a beacon. And the smell, the overpowering scent of fear filling the air lured him as well. He made his way to the farmhouse, but the fear was coming from the barn. Slowly, cautiously, he searched for a way in. Old, weathered wooden planks fastened to cross beams with rusty, worn nails offer little resistance and are easily torn open, granting access to unprotected prey. The hunter howled in triumph.

At 2:02 a.m. Oren Goodman wakes to the monstrous cry. For the second time this week, he grabs his gun and runs outside, but this night is different. This night the sounds are coming from inside the barn. Hideous sounds that Oren has never heard before — the sound of cows screaming. Oren raises his gun. Inch by inch, he moves closer. Timidly, he reaches forward, throws open the barn doors, and stands shocked as half a dozen cows run past him. Two more cows lay on the ground, bleeding from open gashes, trying to get up. A third lies motionless, a monstrous figure looming low over it. Two massive paws hold it down while the creature's head thrashes, its jaw tearing meat from bones. Oren panics and fires too quickly, hitting the cow and sending pieces of cowhide exploding into the air.

The beast snarls a ghastly sound, and all Oren can think is *Run! Run as fast as you can!* His legs go weak but respond to his command. Without thought for anything but his own self-preservation, he runs back toward the house. It is the first time he's run since high school gym class. Muscles dormant for years are now asked to perform like those of an Olympic athlete. Fourteen long strides, feet barely touching the ground, the longest distance of his life. It feels like an eternity, but he makes it to the front door before his legs give out and he falls against the screen door. Throwing it open he grabs the heavy wood edge of the inner door and rushes inside, then slams it closed, throwing his back against it. His legs burn and his hands shake from massive amounts of adrenaline being pumped into his bloodstream. His chest heaves, gasping for breath, inhaling all the stale, musty air from the old farm house.

What was that! What was that? What the FUCK was THAT!! Is all he manages to think before he is paralyzed with fear. The moonlight falling across the floor through the window reveals a black shadow walking upright toward the front door.

Oren hears the scratch of a fingernail or perhaps a claw being dragged across the wood planking outside the house. He jumps away from the door. Standing in the center of the living room, he panics and fires two more rounds: one just left of the window and the other dead center of the front door. The shotgun blast punches two foot-wide circles through the front of his house and fills the room with acrid smoke.

Oren's heart beats out of his chest, as he hopes one of his shots hit its mark, but he's not so lucky. The front porch, visible through the hole in the door, disappears as a mass of black fur eclipses the outside view. Two yellow-green eyes fill the opening and stare deep into Oren's soul. The eyes penetrate, burning into Oren's soon to be, short memory. Massive jaws snap along the edges of the hole. Long, razor-sharp fangs send splinters flying, making the opening wider and wider with every bite. The creature works furiously to get in, scratching and clawing at the hole with one objective: to kill its prey.

Oren raises the gun and squares the sights dead center of the opening, right upon the head, and thinks, *I got you now, you son of a bitch.* He braces for the kickback as he pulls the trigger. The hammer falls upon an empty chamber, and momentary confusion is replaced with fear. He slides the gun's forestock forward and back, chambering another empty round. He pulls the trigger repeatedly, hoping that by some magic a bullet will fly from the barrel and end this nightmare. The beast attacks the ever-widening hole with ferocity. It is only a matter of seconds before he will be able to burst into the house. Oren runs to the gun cabinet, scrambling to find a box of shells. Grabbing a handful of cartridges, he sprints upstairs into his bedroom and locks the door. Here is a small reprieve before the sentence is passed, the verdict is carried out. He grabs the phone and cradles the headset between his ear and neck. A loud crash comes from downstairs. The beast is in. A floorboard creaks and Oren hears the familiar sound of the staircase moan. It is making its way up the stairs … Oren dials 9-1-1.

Rapidly, he jams three shells into the shotgun's loading chamber as he hears Vilma Ortiz say, "Prattsville Sheriff's Department. How can we—"

Oren screams into the phone. *"It's here!"*

Before she can reply, Oren screams his last sentence upon this earth, *"Pete get your ass over here! Now!!!!"*

Oren drops the receiver and backs away from the door, preparing to make his final stand. He waits, not making the same mistake he did downstairs. If this thing cannot unlock doors or turn handles, he just may be safe until Officer Hanlon can get here.

The beast does not bother with door handles or locks. Interior doors, especially ones made when this house was built, were not made to keep four-hundred pounds of animal fury from getting in. The door splinters into pieces, flying toward Oren as the beast comes crashing through. Oren fires blindly, then fires again, where he thinks the creature will be. He is wrong for the last time in his life. The creature rears up and smacks the shotgun from his hands, sending a final round into the ceiling. The creature clamps his jaws down upon Oren's forearm, snapping the ulna and radius bones as if they are toothpicks.

Oren screams and knows one thing for certain: Oren Goodman will be the last male Goodman, and he will die in his ancestral bedroom.

The beast shakes its head and Oren's arm twists at the elbow, ripping bone from joint, severing his arm in half. Oren falls to the floor, grabbing the bloody stump, frantically kicking, trying to get away. The throw rug bunches under his feet as the beast falls to all fours and snaps at his flailing legs. Oren flips, turning his back on the creature, and when he does, the monster's powerful jaws lock onto one of Oren's feet, breaking it at the ankle. Oren screams in pain as the creature claws up his legs, biting and ripping as he goes. Just before Oren loses consciousness, he feels the creature's hot, stinking breath upon his neck. Something wet falls on Oren's head, the drooling beast's saliva dripping from its jaws. The last thing he feels is a stinging pain down his spine. And then he feels nothing.

An unearthly howl reverberates throughout the ancestral home. Officer Hanlon is still thirteen minutes away. Plenty of time for the beast to feast upon its kill before it moves into the night in search of other prey.

Chapter 13
Oren Goodman's Remains

Hanlon speeds through the darkness, pushing the cruiser's engine to its limit. Tires screech, and twice he almost loses control.

"Pete! Pete, come in!" Vilma's voice blares over the noise of the racing engine.

Pete fumbles for the microphone, not taking his eyes off the road. "Vilma, did you get in touch with Oren? Is he …" Pete grabs the steering wheel with both hands, going into a hairpin curve.

Hearing the whole terrible ordeal through the phone's receiver, Vilma cries, "Pete! He's being torn apart … this thing is Killing him!"

Pete gains control and feels for the mic. "I'm three minutes out, call Middleburg and Grand Gorge, send anyone who's not sleeping, and if they are, Wake them up! Call county for an ambulance to meet us there. Try to keep Oren on the line, Vilma. Keep him talking."

"Pete ..." Vilma's voice is soft and mournful. "I think he's dead."

"Just, tell him to hold on!! I'm on my way."

He skids to a stop and slams the gear shifter into park before the car even stops its forward motion. Red and blue lights splash the house as Pete grabs the radio's microphone. Beyond the barn gate, cows are skittishly trotting through the dark meadow.

"I'm here. How far out is the ambulance?"

"About a half-hour," Vilma responds.

Too long. Pete pulls his shotgun from its holder. "I'm going in."

"No! Peter, wait for back-up! Peter! Pete!!!" Vilma's shouts fade the farther he gets from the car. Gingerly, he moves toward the house, focusing the gun's sights on any noises uttering from the darkness. With the car's headlights shining on the house, he spots the hole blown through the front wall of Oren's house and a much larger one torn open in Oren's door. Pete turns and surveys the property, just as his training taught him.

Unwilling to tear his eyes from the moonlit yard, he stumbles backwards to find a step of the front porch. He reaches behind him for the railing, making his way up the stoop until he feels the wooden splinters of the shattered door.

"Oren! You in there?" he shouts, head half-cocked into the open door hole. "Oren!" He listens for any sign of a response.

When none comes, he checks the door handle. Locked. He lifts his leg and snakes his foot into the hole. When his foot touches the floor, he ducks his body through the hole and rapidly fans the gun all around the room until he's satisfied he is alone.

"Oren! It's Officer Hanlon!" He waits again; still no answer. He makes his way to the nearest room, the kitchen. A quick check reveals no movement, no threat. All clear. He moves to the next room. All clear. He is about to move to the next room when a small spot on the tile floor catches his eye. He flicks the light switch on the wall and room floods with light from every lamp positioned around the room. He stands watching the mystery spot, perplexed, trying to register what it is. Then a droplet falls and breaks the surface of the thick, congealed black-reddish spot. Pete stretches his foot forward and tips the toe of his shoe on the edge. He drags his foot back, smearing a crimson streak, and fear clutches his heart.

Slowly he turns his face to the ceiling. There's a large dark stain in the fiberglass drop-ceiling tile, and from it falls another droplet.

"Orennnn!" Pete yells at the top of his lungs. He runs to the base of the stairs before stopping and collecting himself. Step by step he makes his way up the creaky staircase, gun leading the way. At the landing, splintered pieces of Oren Goodman's bedroom door lay scattered about. He points his gun down the hall and waits, listening hard. Satisfied there is no movement in the rest of the house, he turns his attention to the room ahead. A huge part of him does not want to go in, but the police officer in him urges him forward.

"Oren, I'm coming in."

The first thing that hits Pete is the overwhelming smell of death. Pete brings his free hand to his nose and takes one more step before the horror in front of him forces the contents of his stomach to rush from his body. He doubles over, slipping in the thick liquid coving the floor. He thrusts his free hand forward against the wall to steady himself, and feels something warm. He brings his blood-covered palm up and watches as streams of blood run down his forearm, disappearing underneath his shirt sleeve's cuff. In his horror, he drops the shotgun. Blood splashes as it hits the floor. He looks around the room for Oren's body when he realizes Oren Goodman's body is *all around* the room.

It takes him half a second to get downstairs and throw himself out through the front door hole. Two squad cars are pulling into the driveway as his legs give out.

"Don't go in there!" he shouts, before emptying this stomach for the second time.

Chapter 14
Can I Have My Blanket Back?

The sun rises and warms the crisp Catskill mountain air. Jenny sits on the deck while the aroma of freshly ground coffee floods her small one-bedroom apartment. She watches the birth of this new day and wonders what secrets, adventures, hopes, and disappointments this day will bring. The DJ on the radio predicts autumn is on its way, and promises this may be one of the most memorable days of the year. Her thoughts turn to Louis. Actually, her thoughts have not stopped thinking about Louis since their kiss yesterday.

Jenny takes one last sip of coffee and swipes the keys hanging from a hook by the door as she heads to her truck. She's decided she is not going to wait for fate to come to her; she'll be the master of her own destiny. She certainly isn't going to torture herself for an entire month if Louis is leaving today. She needs to know if he feels the same way. After all, he did say he would explain everything today, and last time she checked, 6:47 a.m. was part of today.

Jenny says a prayer, as she does every time she cranks the

engine of her 1995 Chevy Blazer. *One more season baby, I promise.* And like every time before, the American-made Detroit engine roars to life. Jenny smiles and heads down Main Street. The liquor store is only three minutes away, but today the twenty-five-year-old truck is going to travel more than just three minutes. As she leaves town, the not-so-quiet truck wakes the last of the morning sleepers, thanks to the number of holes in the old girl's rusted exhaust.

The engine strains a little as it goes up the slow incline, before much-needed oil lubricates the truck's old and tired parts and the heat kicks in. By the time she reaches her old watering hole, the faithful engine is purring like a kitten and Jenny is singing along with The B-52's "Love Shack." She rounds the school and heads toward Wyckoff Farm. Taking in the view she thinks, *Is there any place better to live than right here?* She turns on to Flat Creek Road and then makes a left onto Maybie Road. Her brothers used to joke, *"Well, is it a road or ain't it?"* and her mother would say, *"Maybe it is and maybe it isn't."*

One day, when she was a little girl, her father had introduced her to Raymond Maybie. "*Whose family the road was named after.*" This man, who looked as old as time, had told her something she'd never forgotten. He'd said, *"Both my father and my father's brother fought at the Battle of Gettysburg, and neither one of them got a scratch. Can you imagine that?"* And all Jenny could think is *"How old are you?"*

Jenny laughs to herself as she comes to the end of Maybie Road. She turns right onto Harrington Road and is heading toward Allen Hill when she spots something on the grassy hilltop off to the right. Lying face up in the meadow, a tan naked figure, like a dark spot on a light sheet of paper, breaks the perfect blanket of green.

Jenny hits the brakes, skidding to the shoulder, and sits mortified. No one ever tells you what to do when you're presented with a dead body. She dials 9-1-1, but there's no service. Now what to do? She could drive to get service, but then what if she comes back and the body is gone? What if the killer has only just dumped the body and is watching her? She quickly hits the door lock button and jumps, as all four doors lock simultaneously. Jenny searches for a weapon and remembers there's a tire iron in the back. The thought, *Okay, you're just gonna go check it out and maybe you'll have better reception on the hilltop,* is quickly followed by *I wonder if news reporters will interview me,* then fear reappears as she wonders, *What if they think I'm the killer?* Shaking off these thoughts, she retrieves the tire iron and proceeds up the hill to where the body lays. The closer she gets, the more sure she is that this was not how she wanted her day to begin. Even from a distant, she can tell it's a man's body. From thirty feet away, the body appears not to be mangled in any way. At twenty-five feet, she sees no signs of gunshot or knife wounds. At fifteen feet away, his head comes into view, and at twelve feet away Jenny stops in horror, realizing she is looking at Louis Kessler.

Jenny runs to Louis's lifeless body and falls to her knees. She drops the tire iron and her phone and shakes him by the shoulders, calling his name. Then she remembers something about not touching a dead body and recoils in fear. She brings her hands to her mouth as a million terrible thoughts flash before her.

Louis blinks and squints. "Jenny?"

"Oh! Louis, are you all right? I thought you were dead!"

"Jenny? What are you doing here?"

"What am I doing *here*? What are *you* doing here?" Jenny thinks, *What an odd question.* "Louis, you're sleeping naked in the middle of a field …" And then it hits her. "Oh! I see what happened. Someone had a bit too much to drink last night and decided to play Nature Boy until he passed out and ended up here!" Jenny collects her things and starts marching to her car.

"Jenny, where are you going?"

"I'm going home!" she yells, "I was coming to see you, but *you* would rather be prancing off in the fields looking for someplace to put your dick into!"

Louis gets up and runs after her, cupping his hands between his legs. "Jenny, wait. It's not like that."

"Oh, it's not? You ran out of the store with a bottle of 'shine so you could get buck naked with God knows who. Well, I hope she was worth it! Good bye, Louis!"

"You can't leave me. I don't even know where I am."

"I don't see how that's any of my concern." She stops and looks at him, momentarily at a loss. His body looks as if Michaelangelo chiseled it out of marble. "Hmm, anyway, why should I help you?"

"Because it would be the decent thing to do? You can't leave me out in the middle of nowhere!" He raises his arms toward the vast countryside around them.

Her eyes trail down. "You have a … point." But then she looks away, shaking her head. "I mean, you have a … ah …" She turns, flushed, lost for words, and wonders, *How could an autumn day be so hot.* "Okay, only because it would be the right thing to do. It has nothing to do with …" She waves her hand as if to shoo a fly away. "Your … situation."

Louis strolls to the truck like he's walking the banks of the Seine River in Paris. Jenny swears a part of him is enjoying watching her embarrassment.

"Aren't you cold? I'm mean, it doesn't appear to have an affect on your … ah, I mean you."

"You know, Jenny, the Royal British Navy does cold-weather training in sub-zero conditions. They jump into a frozen lake in Estonia, where temperatures sometimes reach twenty below. The only way to stop from freezing to death is to run three miles until your body temperature warms up."

Jenny smirks. "So, you're telling me you're part of the British Royal Navy, and you were just out for a run last night and decided to take a nap?"

"Well, no, not exactly," he says, rubbing his head.

"Maybe you'd prefer running alongside, flapping in the wind." Again she waves her hand, this time hanging low, resembling an elephant's trunk. "While I sit in a nice warm truck?"

Louis responds, embarrassed. "Just making conversation."

She stops at the back of the Blazer and retrieves an old blanket she keeps there. "Here." She shoves the blanket against his chest. "Wouldn't want your little British Officer to die from exposure."

Louis sits wrapped in a cocoon of soft cotton with just his head emerging.

"I should have let you sit there butt naked," Jenny says, breaking the awkward silence. Then she smiles a devilish grin. "You're lucky it's not summer."

He flaps the blanket's edges. "So I'm guessing, judging by how you keep a blanket in the truck, I'm not the first naked man you've had sitting here?" Louis jokes.

"No, Louis. I'm not in the habit of driving around, finding naked men, and taking them home!" she retorts with hostility.

"I'm just trying to—"

"I know what you're just trying to do, and how many naked

men I have driven around in my truck is the last thing I would be bringing up right about now." She snaps, as they come upon Louis's abandoned truck outside his gate. She throws Louis a disappointed look, much like a mother who's been called down to the principal's office.

"Don't get up, I got this. The code?" Jenny gets out.

"8211981," Louis recites.

"And the keys?" she calls out, walking away.

"They should be in the truck," he shouts as she tucks her head into the driver's side window, checking. She picks up the empty bottle of moonshine and tosses it in the back of Louis's truck with another disappointed look. She punches in the seven-digit code as Louis yells the numbers a little slower. The gate swings open. After she drives Louis's truck through and parks it on the side of the dirt drive, Jenny walks back to the Blazer. The jalopy limps through before the gate swings shut.

"If my truck breaks down on this road, I'm taking yours," Jenny declares as the two of them bounce around inside the cab.

"You said you were coming to see me. Why?" Louis asks.

"I wanted to know why we can't be together." She gives him a look that no man ever wants to see on the face of someone they care about. "But I think I've found my answer."

"Jenny, I wish I could tell you" —his eyes are sincere— "but I just can't. All I can tell you is that it's best I'm alone."

"Louis, I'll be honest with you. You're someone I thought I could care about, maybe I still do." She looks at him sympathetically. "I see a lost puppy and I have this need to help it."

"Florence Nightingale Syndrome," Louis interjects.

"Florence what now?"

"It's the clinical term for caregivers who fall in love with their patients."

"Whoa! No one said I'm falling in love with you! Boy, the ego on some people." She shakes her head. "All I'm saying is, I wanted to get to know you, but if you're planning on drinking yourself to death, I don't want to know you! Hell, by all means, get shit-faced and stumble off into the frozen woods. I'll even drop you off right here." She stops the truck a hundred yards before his cabin. "You can hand me my blanket and carry on with your little siesta." She looks him dead in the eyes. "I'll turn the truck around, head home, and never give you a second thought."

"That's not what I want," Louis snaps. "In fact, that's why I come up here … to stop from killing myself."

She looks at him, bewildered. "You said you have a disease?"

"It's more like a condition … I was born with it."

"You said it wasn't something I could catch?"

"That's right. I inherited it from my father. It can only be passed down through birth. Most of the time it's dormant, but when I have an attack, it's excruciating. That's why I drink. Drinking helps."

"So that's why you don't want to be with me?"

"I didn't say that … I'm just used to being alone. I've gotten used to it." He hangs his head. "It's just easier this way."

She puts her hand on his exposed shoulder, "Oh my god, Louis, you're freezing."

This suddenly reminds Louis of his nakedness and he asks, "Would you mind if we continue this conversation when I have more clothing on?"

She guns the truck up the dirt road.

Once at the cabin, her motherly instincts kick in again and she helps him through his door. "First thing we're gonna do is get you into a nice hot shower." She raises an eyebrow as if to ask the question, *where is the bathroom?*

"Oh. Right through there." He points to the smaller door in the far corner.

Steam fills the bathroom as she adjusts the showerhead. She turns to Louis, "Let's get you in."

Louis gives her a look, still wrapped in the oversized blanket.

"Louis, I've seen naked men before … I've seen *you* naked."

"I'm a big boy, Jenny. I can take it from here."

"I know you are," she smiles; a double entendre giggle escapes her. She holds out her hand. "Well, can I at least have my blanket back?"

"You're not going to be happy until you see me naked one more time?" he jokes.

"I saved your life. It's the least you can do."

Louis unwraps the soft cotton blanket from his body, feeling like a cliché Valentine's day present. Somewhere in his head, a clarinet plays David Rose's "The Stripper."

Jenny smiles.

Louis emerges from a steam-filled bathroom wearing only a towel, ready for catcalls and whistles. Instead, he finds a lone shoe, followed by a sock, and then the other shoe, followed by its matching sock. A trail of clothes leads to his bedroom. A pair of jeans, then a shirt. Black satin panties and finally, a black lace bra hanging from the doorknob. Louis slowly opens the door, nervous and anxious about what waits for him on the other side.

"Hello," he calls into the dimly lit room.

The door creaks open, filling the room with light. Jenny stands wrapped in her soft cotton blanket. The edges just meeting in the front, creating a valley of soft skin all the way down to her navel.

"I figured, I saw *you* naked." She lets the blanket slide from her skin. It forms a small mountain at the base of her legs, "It's only proper you get to see me … naked."

Louis closes the door.

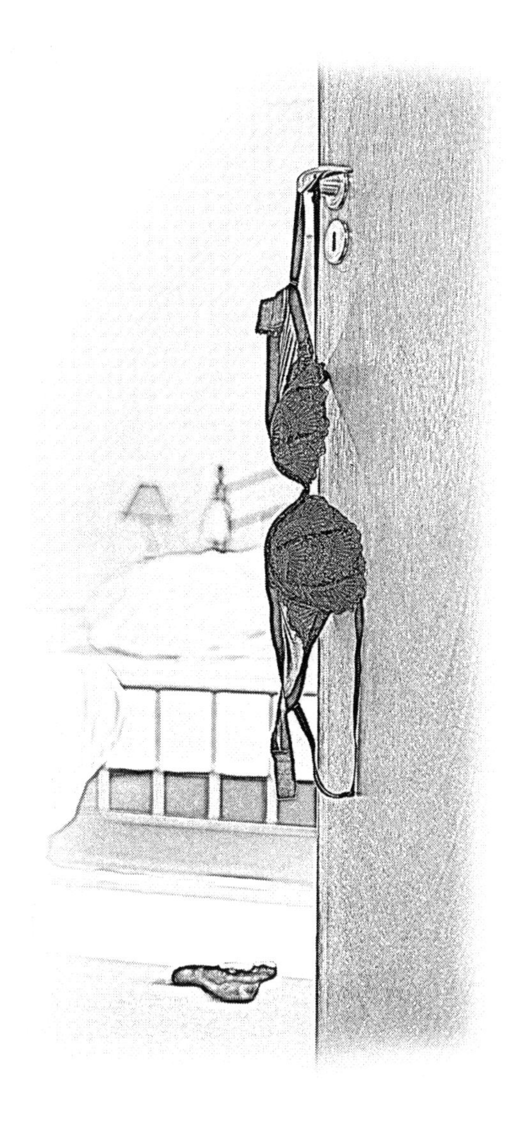

Chapter 15
Have You Ever Seen Tracks Like These?

The same sun that rose and warmed Jenny's morning also rises for Officer Hanlon. And for certain, the memorable day predicted on the radio will live in the memories of every person of the Schoharie County Law enforcement agency. Four and a half hours before dawn, Officer Hanlon was barking out orders to secure the house and barn and flood the area with as many searchlights as they had. Three hours ago, the Margaretville ambulance crew left and was replaced by a van from the Albany Coroner's Office. Officer Hanlon's night has been one long stream of horror since 3 o'clock in the morning, with endless questions he has no answers to.

Over the course of the past four hours, every officer has asked him the same stupid questions. "What the hell happened here? Did you see anything? Do you know what did this?" But most of them just mumble "Jesus Christ."

In those same four hours, officers from every surrounding

county have arrived. Warned by earlier-arriving officers not to go inside, yet filled with testosterone, they enter the house with chests puffed out, claiming they've seen everything from highway collisions to deer mutilations and nothing affects them. Then, just like the ones before them, upon exiting the house —sometimes running, sometimes stumbling— they throw up in front of the squad car.

As the sun breaks over the hills, Officer Hanlon orders the lights turned off and instructs the men to begin a more thorough investigation of the property. "I want anything you can find, a footprint, a hair sample, a spot of blood, any" —he's about to say *any bit or piece left of Oren,* but stops himself— "any evidence at all, I want it!"

As the medical examiner walks toward him. Pete thinks, *If he asks me the same fucking questions, I'm going to lose it.*

"Officer Hanlon? I'm Inspector Macaluso, Albany Coroner's office. We're almost done in there. Do you know—"

"No! I don't know who, or what, killed him! He was like that when I got here! Okay!"

Inspector Macaluso musters an understanding smirk. "What I was going to say was, do you know if he had any family we can contact?"

Hanlon shakes his head and hangs it low. "Sorry. It's just, I've been answering stupid questions all night. Been up since, shit, I don't know when I slept last. Sorry, no, Oren had no other family. This place was all he ever knew. Always said he'd die here. I guess he never thought it would be like this."

"It's all right, officer. Go home. Get some rest."

Any other day, exhaustion might set in, but after what Pete's seen, a peaceful night's sleep may never come for him again. "No can do."

He looks around. "You have any idea what we're dealing with? I mean, who could have done this?"

"Judging from the mess in the barn, I would say it was a pack of ravenous carnivores. But the strange part is, it looks like the work of only one animal."

"One animal?"

"Your killer was a large carnivore with abnormally large incisors judging by these bite marks. Either that or you have a lunatic on your hands who made instruments to simulate teeth and claws."

"Why would someone do that?"

"Believe me, I've seen a lot weirder things in this line of work. But I'm guessing it's some kind of animal. It looks like it took down two cows before feeding on a third. I'm thinking that's when Mr. Goodman interrupted the creature's feeding. He shot the hell out of the cow. Maybe aiming at the thing and missed, maybe to put the cow out of its misery? Who knows … but I'm thinking he pissed it off and it came after him."

Pete's face twists into a grotesque expression, looking at the barn.

"Here, let me show you something." Inspector Macaluso walks him into the house and stops before going up the stairs. "You notice anything?"

Pete looks around. "Besides the huge hole in the door and the one in the wall? No."

Macaluso smiles. "I do. We're trained to see things most people overlook." He points out bloody shoeprints smudged on the stairs, heading out the door.

"Yeah, those are mine, so?"

"Precisely. Those are yours. So why are there no tracks from the animal that killed him? Certainly, a crime this heinous, the animal would have gotten blood all over him. So where are his paw prints? How did he get out of the house?" Macaluso motions to Pete to follow, "Mind your shoeprints, please." He carefully steps on every other step to avoid contaminating the evidence. They reach the bedroom.

"Now here's where you came in, and here's where you fell, and your gun dropped there, which made the splatter print on the wall over there. Which was hard to distinguish with all the other blood splatter, but I think we have a pretty accurate picture of what happened."

Pete looks at the forensic analysis of his onetime friend and can't believe how terrifying it was hours before, only now to hear it described like a missed field goal by a Friday night sports announcer.

"Whatever kind of animal it was, it broke down the door, Mr. Goodman fired off two rounds, here and here." Macaluso points to large holes in the wall. "A third one up there, assuming the gun was deflected, before whatever it was overpowered him and wrestled him to the ground. It's there that he proceeded to use some sort of sharp object to dismember Mr. Goodman, for reasons we still do not know."

"Were you able to …" Pete motions around the room with the same grotesque look on his face, "… you know, find all of him?"

Macaluso frowns and tactfully says, "Let's just say it's going to be a closed casket."

Pete looks around the room, aghast that every section, fragment, particle, and scrap of the person who used to be Oren Goodman has been removed, leaving only deep crimson stains soaking into the weathered floorboards and antiquated throw rugs.

"Here's why there were no tracks leaving the room." Macaluso tiptoes across the bedroom, being careful not to disturb anything.

"The creature broke the window out to escape."

"You mean it broke the window?"

"No, Hanlon, the animal broke the window OUT." He waves around the entire frame where the window would be, "If it simply broke the windowpanes, the frame and everything around it should still be intact. This creature broke through the window, taking the glass, the frame, the molding, and most of the surrounding wall, as well as some of the exterior boards. This animal is exceptionally bulky."

Pete walks across the room, and Macaluso cringes as he blatantly disregards safeguarding the evidence.

Pete sticks his head out the window. Glass and wood debris litters the small roof covering the porch and farther down, to the ground below. Pete signals to a group of officers standing around talking. "Thompson, O'Connor."

Two officers walk toward him and Officer Hanlon waves them off frantically, then shakes his head, knowing it's too late.

"Yeah, Chief?"

"You see those pieces of glass and wood splinters below your feet?" They both look down, then up at the smashed-out window. "Well, that's what we call evidence! And you two dip-shits are standing in it!" He shouts as they jump back, trying to avoid the already trampled area.

Both Hanlon and Macaluso hurry downstairs to the back of the house, where Thompson and O'Connor are taping off the area with yellow Crime Scene tape.

Hanlon throws the two officers a look that could kill and shakes his head as he bypasses the tape and studies the well-traveled ground. There are several large boot prints, trampled over by a couple of dozen shoeprints Hanlon figures were made by earlier officers searching the property. Shattered glass and splintered wood fragments have been ground in to the mud and dirt, along with any evidence that may have been there.

"Son of a b—" Hanlon yells and smacks the evidence tape out of Thompson's hands. "Little late for that! The entire crime scene is tainted! Hell! A man died up there. Maybe you want to get him two aspirins and a drink of water while you're at it!"

He explores the ground, shaking his head. "Could have been here … could have been right here. We could have got some kind of imprint that would identify what kind of animal this was, but now … Aarggggg! It's all shit!"

Ready to unleash fire and brimstone upon the two naïve officer, Pete is interrupted, when a reprieve comes from another younger officers who calls out, "Officer Hanlon! I think I found something!"

Macaluso follows closely behind as the two of them race to the front of the house.

"We missed it in the darkness, but now that the sun is up …" The young trooper points to the wooden planks on the porch. "I figure whatever killed the cows in the barn must have stepped in something as it made its way to the front door."

Pete looks over his shoulder to Thompson and O'Connor, who have followed hesitantly. "At least *someone* around here is thinking!"

"Anyway, I thought you had a wolf … an extremely large wolf, but here's something I can't figure out." The young trooper points out a partial print and then another a stride away, and then one more.

"You thought it was a wolf?" Macaluso says.

"Well, yeah. Just look!" The trooper looks at them and then points at some kind of huge, but indistinguishable animal print. "Could be a bear. Looks somewhat like a wolf but can't possibly be one. It's way too big."

"It's not a bear!" Pete snaps, hearing himself utter the exact words Oren spoke less than twenty-four hours ago. Red, blue, and white flashing strobe lights assault Officer Hanlon, painting the house and surrounding trees with a constant rhythmic reminder of the gruesome crime scene. He storms off to his cruiser and yells to anyone within earshot, "For God's sake, can you people PLEASE turn off these damn flashing strobe lights. It looks like a fucking nightclub for cops out here!"

Macaluso follows, like he's a small child trying to catch up to his fast-moving parents. "Where are you going?"

"To question the person who may be harboring this animal on his land!"

Macaluso shrugs. "Am I missing something? Why couldn't it be a wolf?"

Pete opens the door to the cruiser and stops, stupefied. "The tracks," he finally says in a murmur.

Macaluso shakes his head. "What about them?"

Pete gets in and starts the engine. Before slamming the gear shift into drive he says, in disbelief, "The stride. Whatever made those tracks was walking upright."

Chapter 16
Good Friends Never Die

A thin layer of sweat covers Louis's body. Filled with all the vitality of a high school track star only moments ago, he now lies on his back, gasping for air. The large amounts of dopamine that urged his body forward have left, leaving him immobilized and aching. There are thirty parts of the brain that are activated during an orgasm. Right now, Louis can't access any of them.

In contrast, Jenny looks like a kitten intertwined amongst the soft white comforter and bedsheets. A look of pure content dances in her eyes as she playfully twists and shifts in the sea of bedding. Her hand lazily falls upon his abdomen and bobs along with his rhythmic panting. He cannot remember the last time he was with a woman, and it's for this reason he's wanted to make a lasting impression. He turns and kisses the nape of her neck.

"You ready to go again?" she says in jest, sensing one more time would require an ambulance to the mountaintop.

Louis bursts out in a conceding laugh. "I was thinking more

like something to eat. You want to try an authentic, traditional English breakfast?"

"What's in a traditional English breakfast?"

"It's bacon, sausages, eggs, tomatoes, mushrooms, toast, and beans." He raises and walks over to the dresser. "You do eat meat, don't you?" which, after he said it, sounded inappropriate.

She tilts her head and gives him a look as if to say, *I live in upstate New York, cow country,* but instead the look comes across like, *After what we just did?*

"I mean you're not a vegetarian or—"

She stops him with a cute little chuckle. "Bacon would be nice. Oh, but can I have my eggs over easy?"

"Over easy? See, all these things I'm learning about you." He smiles as he pulls up his pants and throws on a T-shirt. "Usually the chef doesn't allow substitutions, but I believe he's in an especially good mood this morning, I think you're in luck."

She raises her eyebrow. "Oh, he better be."

He stops at the door and looks at her. She sinks into the center of the bed, pulling the covers over her. *This could be a pleasant life,* he thinks.

With his hand draped over the doorknob, he begins to drag the door closed as he turns to leave the room.

A familiar voice expresses a morning greeting, "Hello, Louis."

"Aaaagh!" Louis yells, jumping back against the door, knocking it open and staggering into the bedroom.

"Are you all right?" Jenny yells, bolting upright in bed.

"Yeah, yeah, I just … I saw one of your socks and thought it was a rat," he lies.

"A rat!"

"Well, maybe a large mouse," he corrects.

She slumps back into bed laughing. "If that's how you react

to seeing a mouse, Louis, I hate to see what happens when you see a spider. Oh, Louis, can you get my clothes? I'm not quite the exhibitionist you are … or are you a nudist?" Her laughter disappears as he closes the door.

"What are you doing here?" Louis turns to his unwanted guest as he begins to pick up the trail of clothes.

"Really, Louis, I'm getting a little offended by your reaction every time you see me."

"You can't blame me. Have you seen yourself lately? You haven't aged well."

The thing standing before Louis turns and looks into a mirror. His head turns from side to side, up and down, to see every angle. A rotting hand reaches up and caresses an exposed portion of his mandible with the bony tip of an index finger held in place only by dried-up tendons. On the other side of his decaying face, an empty hole where his nose used to be connects to the bright white angular cheek bone by a small crescent-shaped crevice in his gray, decomposing flesh. "I see what you mean."

Louis gives him a disgusted look. "Why are you here?"

"Do you have any idea what you did?"

Louis pauses near the bedroom door. A memory burned into his brain plays out before him. A warm feeling washes over him and he smiles as he retrieves Jenny's bra from the doorknob. "I have a pretty good idea."

He opens the door and places her clothes on the chair beside the door. Jenny is savoring the last few moments of solitude before having to get up. Louis closes the door, stealing a fleeting glimpse.

"Not that, Louis. What *you* did last night."

"I … I couldn't get in, then I tried …" He makes his way to the kitchen, hits the button on the coffeemaker, and takes a carton of eggs and butter from the refrigerator. He moves to the stove.

"Yes, Louis, you tried, but you didn't. For the first time in a long time, you thought about it. Hell, you even put your mind to it and took steps, but what happened?"

A blue flame ignites under a frying pan, and a pat of butter melts. "There was no electricity," Louis says shamefully and thinks, *I have to speak to Jim about that.*

"Then what did you do?"

"I … I …" Louis's hands shake. He closes his eyes. "I don't remember."

"Shall I tell you?"

"Please, just go away," he exhales, barely audible. He buries his face in his trembling hands.

"Remember when you first came to me?"

"Yes, and you didn't believe me. You thought it was all in my head! *You* said you could help me."

"I've already apologized for that. I was wrong, Louis."

"Yeah, *you* were *wrong*! And I'm reminded of it every time I see you."

"I'm sorry if my appearance disturbs you, Louis. I see you still haven't taken responsibility for your own actions."

"I took responsibility. I'm up here; I haven't harmed anyone since" —he pauses and stares at the thing— "well, since you."

"Until now, Louis."

"No," Louis cries in a whisper.

"Louis, I want you to meet someone …"

"Please, no. No, please. I'm begging you," Louis pleads, rocking back and forth. "Just go away!" he screams.

"Louis, this is Mr. —"

"KESSLER, it's Officer Hanlon! Open the gate!" An electronic voice suddenly floods the room, startling Louis more than his present company.

Louis throws the spatula into the sink. "Terrific! This is all I need!" He turns off the stove and walks over to the monitoring station.

Jenny opens the bedroom door, standing there in his bathrobe. "I hope you're not telling me to go away?"

"Oh! No, I was … It's …" he looks at Jenny with a stern look. "You look beautiful."

"Don't change the subject. I heard you talking to someone. You told me to go away!"

"Kessler!" Officer Hanlon's disembodied voice calls out again.

"What the hell is that?" Jenny frantically scans every corner of the cabin.

"We have a visitor." Louis presses a combination of keys on his security's keypad unlocking the main entrance. He gestures toward the surveillance monitor which shows Officer Hanlon's cruiser slowly edging its way through the gate.

"As much as I don't want you to, you have to put on some clothes. We're going to have company in about …" In a smaller window on the monitor, Louis sees the cruiser's tires kicking back loose gravel as the car speeds with determination. "I would say, less than a minute, judging by the way he's attacking that road."

Jenny turns as she closes the bedroom door, says, "This isn't over."

CHAPTER 17
IT COULD HAVE BEEN YOU

Officer Hanlon has raced to Louis Kessler's main gate over the hill, which means he's had to take several out-of-the-way roads. *Jeez, it would have been easier to drive over the mountain from the old Karney place,* he thinks. For the first time in eight hours, Pete is alone with his thoughts with only the hum of the tires and the groan of the engine. Over and over, images of last night's horror flash through his brain. *Jesus, what could have done that? What kind of animal has Kessler unleashed up here?* He slows as the entrance comes into view. Kessler's truck is on the other side of the gated boundary. Stopping at the call box, he picks up the car's microphone and switches on the loudspeaker.

"Kessler. You out there!" Pete's voice projects to the surrounding area and echoes off the hills. "Kessler!" He waits, but only briefly, then hits the call button on the keypad of the call box. "Kessler, It's Officer Hanlon! Open the gate!" His patience running low, he holds down the call button and shouts, "Kessler!"

Seconds later, a buzzing sound is followed by a metallic clank and the gate swings open. Pete clears the gate and attacks the dirt road faster than a Baja racer flying over dunes in Mexico. Rocks fly from the back of his cruiser and a dust cloud forms in the air. A row of pine trees lines the last fifty yards of the path, then he sees the cabin in a clearing overlooking the valley. The sight of an all-too-familiar Chevy Blazer hits him like a sucker punch to the gut. "That's just fucking great." Pete hits his siren twice to announce his presence before he parks and gets out.

Louis is holding the screen door open to meet him, "Morning, Officer. What brings you around this early?"

"Cut the crap, Kessler. Mind if I come in?" He spews in a sarcastic tone, squeezing by Louis as if to assert his dominance, expecting to see Jenny.

"Okay," Louis whispers to himself, letting the screen door spring closed. He projects his voice louder. "Can I get you a cup of coffee?"

"Listen, Kessler, this is no social call. Just what the hell are you doing up here?"

Images of Jenny wrestling with him under the sheets are the only thing that comes to mind. Louis doubts what he and Jenny have done is a criminal offense. *Well, maybe in some parts of Arkansas?* he thinks with a smirk, but quickly extinguishes his smile.

"I'm sorry, I'm a little unsure of the question? What am I doing here?" He points to the floor. "Should I not be here? Or do you mean, as in living here? In *your* town?"

"I'm in no mood for bullshit right now, Kessler." Hanlon takes off his hat and moves around the cabin. "A person was killed last night! Someone I knew, and I've spent the last eight hours at the scene, then watched as the coroner took his body away or what was left of it."

"And you think I did it?" Louis asks nervously.

"No, but now that you mention it, where were you last night?"

"He was with me," Jenny calls from the bedroom doorway. She moves toward the kitchen and pours two cups of coffee. Louis furrows his brow. *Why would she say that?*

"Who died?" she asks, retrieving a carton of milk from the refrigerator and pouring a little in one cup.

"Oren Goodman," Pete says mournfully.

She walks over and hands the creamed coffee to Hanlon; a kind of peace offering that he takes instinctively. An overpowering sense of sadness takes over him as he quickly chokes back tears.

"You can't possibly think Louis did it. Do you?" she asks.

"Highly unlikely." He stares into the coffee, thinking, *How nice it would be coming home to Jenny.* Then he returns to the business at hand. "We're looking for some kind of animal. That's why I came here." He turns to Louis, using a less aggressive tone. "I need to know just what kind of animals you're bringing on to your property."

"You think my deer are killing people?"

"Not deer, but maybe you're keeping something on this property that may not be legal. And maybe this thing got out last night and—"

"And attacked Mr. Goodman?" Jenny jumps in. "Did you ever think maybe Mr. Goodman got trampled by his own cows?"

"Jenny, he was …" Pete pauses, searching for a delicate way of telling her. "He had bite marks."

"Maybe coyotes?" she counters.

"Jenny, he was …" Knowing she's not going to stop until he gives a full description, he tries one last time to be tactful. "He was mangled."

"Maybe he got between a black bear and her cubs," she contends.

"Jenny!" He bangs the coffee mug on the table forcefully, like a judge gaveling a court to order. "He was ripped apart in his bedroom!" Seeing her shock, he struggles to return his voice to normal. "He called me, saying something was after him … I heard it. It was no bear! I saw … I saw what was left of him—what little was left."

He turns to Louis, only now he speaks in not so nice a tone, perhaps aggravated that Jenny has made him relive what happened. "That's why I need to know everything you've brought onto this land. And you can expect a visit from the game warden as well."

Louis walks over to a small desk and begins writing. When he's done, he hands a slip of paper to Pete. "Those are all the animals I've purchased since I bought the property. I've included the names of the people I got them from and their phone numbers. I've also written my number in New York if you need to get in touch with me, as well as the security code if you'd like to search the grounds when I'm not here."

Officer Hanlon glances at the paper and takes a mental inventory. *Pigs, chickens, couple of dozen goats, deer and a black bear.*

"You brought a black bear up here?" he asks, as if to say, *Why didn't you tell me this sooner?*

"The bear died some time back … hence the reason for the fence. I believe there were poachers. I can give you the game warden's report, if you'd like?" He starts back toward the desk.

Pete waves him off, disappointed. "Won't be necessary. Nothing on here could have done … well, the damage that was at the scene." He picks up his hat. "I would like to search the grounds."

Louis nods. "By all means, anything I can do to help. I'll be away most of the month, but I'll be back—"

"Twenty-somewhat days," Jenny interrupts.

Pete looks at Jenny. "Thanks for the coffee. I'll talk to you later."

He tips his hat at Louis. "Normally, I would say don't leave town, but in this case …" He gives Louis a look as if to say, *I insist you leave.* "I'll be back, you know, to search the grounds."

They listen to the sound of the cruiser leaving before Jenny turns to Louis. An icy shiver snakes up his back from the look she is giving him. "Jenny, you *don't* think I …"

She runs into his arms and holds him tight. "Louis, you were out there last night …"

"Jenny, he said it was some kind of—"

"I know! You were drunk off your ass out there with that thing running around. Louis! It could have been *you* that was killed last night."

Chapter 18
22 Days Later

Louis negotiates the twists and turns of the Taconic State Parkway with both anticipation and trepidation. The farther away from the city he travels, the more a sense of calm washes over him, like slowly walking into the warm waters of the Caribbean. The full green trees of the Outer Boroughs, however sparse, metamorphose into vibrant colors found only in a child's crayon drawing. Bight-colored trees line the banks of the asphalt roadway; a blanket of copper leaves covers the last dying grass blades of summer. As he makes his way farther north, closer to the small town of Prattsville, the autumn trees give up their sunset-colored foliage, until here the trees show only barren limbs. The once overgrown woods of upstate New York now stand bare with bony, twisted skeleton fingers stretching upwards toward the ever-cloudy, pale-gray sky. It is a time when the forest reveals its hidden secrets, as long-forgotten dwellings peek through the tree's timbers, revealed by the loss of brush or overgrown weeds.

Louis's mind is a jumble of thoughts, wondering what awaits him in the small hamlet. Based upon seemingly endless phone calls from Officer Hanlon, Louis has ascertained no other evidence, besides a smeared animal pawprint that cannot be identified, was found at the scene. What is even more troubling to Louis, as Officer Hanlon has explained on the phone, is there have been no other attacks, not even a report of an animal stalking livestock, *not since you left town.*

The fact that Officer Hanlon thinks he somehow could be involved in something so horrendous frightens Louis to his core.

The news of Oren Goodman's death shocked the entire upstate community, and rumors spread like wildfire from town to town. By the time it reached Syracuse, the tale had grown into an attack by a lunatic grizzly bear with a new strain of rabies that broke into a church and devoured a farmer. And now, all of Upstate was unnerved by stories of a crazed bear making its way across the Adirondacks. For the people of Prattsville, however, the story has transformed into something of a Hollywood picture show. Louis cannot believe the stories Jenny's told him, but apparently guns have been flying off the shelves and game wardens have been inundated with questions about the consequences of shooting a crazed animal. There's even a reward posted, but the description is vague:

WANTED DEAD!
EXTREMELY LARGE CREATURE
RESPONSIBLE FOR THE
DEATH OF OREN GOODMAN.

Louis slows the car to a crawl as he nears the town. He feels everyone's eyes upon him, even though no one is on the streets. The once quaint town remains gripped by fear by the event that transpired just before Louis left. Random sheets of paper intermingle with swirling patches of leaves dancing across the street, reminiscent of the ghost towns of the Old West. He forgoes the customary trip to the grocery store and heads directly to the liquor store.

Tiny bells alert everyone inside, and Louis's lighthearted mood is quickly snuffed out by the frigid blank stares of Jenny's customers.

"Morning, Jenny. How's your—" The word "mother" gets stuck in Louis's throat as Jenny's eyes beg for him to fade into the melancholy sea which engulfs the store. Louis muddles around the store, picking up bottles and returning them to the shelves; killing time until the last customer finally exits the shop.

Jenny walks out from behind the counter and heads to the back room. Louis maneuvers through the aisles, heading her off. "Jenny, what's going on …"

"Not here." She grabs his arm and walks him into the small room at the back of the shop. Once there, she throws herself in his arms, taking Louis by surprise. "Oh, Louis! It's been terrible around here." Tears fill her eyes. "Oren's funeral was the hardest thing this town ever endured."

Louis wraps his arms around her and holds her tight. He can feel her quivering. The slight trembling reverberates straight into his core.

"Shhh, it's going to be all right," is all he can manage.

"Even when Hurricane Irene came through here and almost wiped this town off the map, the town rose up and joined together, and there was a feeling of community. But now … oh, Louis, now everyone is terrified, and it's just getting worse."

He rubs her arms, trying to calm and comfort her. A flood of emotions held back for three long weeks breaks the dam, sending a stream of tears running down her face as she gasps for air between sobs. "Pete said there wasn't even enough of Oren to piece together. It was so sad, not even a current photo of him. The only pictures the funeral parlor could find were old photos of him when he was a boy." Her tears come harder. "All I can see is that small boy, just waiting to grow up only to be … to be …" The words never come, only endless laments.

Tiny bells ring out front and Jenny jumps back quickly, wiping her eyes and trying to compose herself. She sniffles into a tissue she keeps with her for moments like these when her emotions erupt.

Louis ducks his head through the doorway and calls, "She'll be right with you."

"How do I look?" she asks.

"Like an angel," he blurts, not thinking.

Her chin jerks back into her neck; a frown creeps down her cheeks.

"I mean like a princess!" He quickly changes his answer and repeats, "A princess! You look like a princess!"

She shoots forward in a burst of laughter and then smiles, looking up as she passes him on the way out of the back room. "Really, Louis? A princess? That's what you came up with?" She giggles to herself. "Like Ariel, or Snow White?"

She turns back to him. "Thanks, Louis. I needed a good laugh."

A princess? What was I thinking? He shakes his head.

Out in the shop he hears Jenny say, "Mr. Hutchins, what can I get for you? Your usual wine?"

○❩❩❩●❨❨❨○

Louis emerges just as Mr. Hutchins is leaving, but not before he throws Louis a cross look. "What the hell was that for?"

"Don't let it get to you, Louis. People are cautious of anyone not from around here since Mr. Goodman's death. I'm afraid fear has made this town not so friendly."

"Well, I was hoping to take you out for dinner tonight." Through the window, Louis sees Officer Hanlon crossing the parking lot. "Unless you have plans?"

"Oh no, of course, I would love to."

Louis smiles, and if not for the inevitable interruption from Officer Hanlon, he might have kissed her. "Great. I'll pick you up at seven?"

Jenny fires back quickly. "Can we make it earlier? I don't want to get back too late."

A perplexed look crosses Louis's face. "What? Is it *American Idol* night? Oh. Please don't tell me you watch *The Bachelorette*? You know they're all actors, right?"

"Louis, that thing is still out there."

Louis smiles sadly.

Jenny punches his chest. "The whole town is on edge."

Right on cue, the small metal bells ring as Officer Hanlon steps through the door. Louis and Jenny stare like a pair of deer caught in a car's headlights at the unwanted intruder. Hanlon closes the door slowly, never taking his eyes off the two. His detective skills kick into overdrive, as if he's just caught two lovers conspiring to kill their spouses.

"Morning, Jenny." He smiles then turns to Louis, the corners of his lips turn down sternly. "Mr. Kessler."

Both return greetings. Louis leaves, but before reaching where Pete is standing he calls out defiantly, "Okay, I'll see you tonight," never blinking under Officer Pete's gaze.

"Don't you want your bottle of scotch?" Jenny asks.

"No. I don't need it tonight." He addresses Pete. "Any progress with the case?"

Pete shakes his head. "Not yet." Then he adds an extra dig. "It's like the killer just up and disappeared." He turns and follows Louis as he passes. "Perhaps, in the next couple of days, something will present itself to us?"

Louis knows full well what he means, but plays it cool. "Good luck with that."

As soon as Louis leaves, Pete pounces like a jaguar, verbally attacking Jenny. "I don't want you seeing him!"

Jenny's mind races and without thinking she cries, "What!"

"*You* heard me. I don't want you seeing him!" he retorts in an even sterner tone.

A look of disgust appears on Jenny's face, and she returns fire like any woman would. "What are *you,* my father?" Her hands anchor to her hips in opposition, waiting for him to open his mouth.

"I'm just saying—" is all he is able to get out before she unloads a barrage of protests.

"First of all, *no*! You are not my father. Second, are you my boyfriend? *Again no*!" She moves around the small shop, straightening bottles and gathering discarded cardboard scraps. "Third, I don't remember asking your opinion, on *who* I can date, or is going out with someone at my age somehow against the law in Schoharie County? I don't think so." She throws the handful of scraps into the back room. "So tell me, Officer Pete …" She stresses his name, more of an insult than his title. "How is it *any* of your business what I do?"

She spins, one eye squinting, head cocked just enough to hide the right side of her face, like she's a gunfighter poised to pull a six-shooter from a holster. *Your move, Black Bart.*

Pete moves cautiously with both hands raised, as he has been trained to do when dealing with drug addicts or the criminally insane. "I'm just trying to look out for you, Jenny." He sees a second assault coming and quickly adds, "Look, Jenny, I have no problem with you dating anyone you want." There's a moment of hesitation before the second wave and he seizes the opening. "All I'm asking is that you be careful when it comes to Louis Kessler." He lowers his hands. "You may not want to hear this, but I did some digging on your friend. Did you know he spent time in an institution?"

Her expression changes to one of bewilderment.

"And not a higher education institution. He was seeing a psychiatrist after his mother was killed when he was a teenager."

She quickly snaps back. "I'm sure your mother dying would mess up any kid."

"She didn't just die, Jenny. She was killed."

"Murdered?"

"No. Not murder; they labeled it an accident. Some kind of animal attack." His eyes widen. "An *animal* attack, Jenny!"

"Okay, that is weird, but I'm sure lots of people would talk to therapists after something like that happened."

"Jenny ..." he says as calmly as he can, "his therapist was also killed." He wants to stop when he sees her shocked expression, but then feels she needs to hear the rest. "He was attacked too. All I could find out from the police report was that it happened in the middle of the night at his house, by what was described as a large dog."

Chapter 19

Twenty-Four Years Earlier

A Terrible Night

The year is 1997. All of England is mourning the death of Princess Diana, except a sixteen-year-old boy who mourns his own mother's death. A much younger Louis Kessler sits in a police station in Northern England, sobbing. His hands shake uncontrollably as patches of his mother's blood dry to his skin and stain his clothes.

"Is that the boy?" a groggy, quickly dressed, disheveled gentleman asks the detective.

"Louis Kessler. He found his mum. She was dead when he found her. It appears to have been some sort of animal attack."

"And the boy's father?"

"Died before the boy was born. Never in the picture."

"I see. Mind if I talk with him?"

"Not at all. That's why we've called you here, Doctor. He just keeps mumbling 'it's his fault.' He blames himself. This kind of thing can put one off his trolley for life. Can you help him?"

The man smirks. "I'll give it a go," he says, and walks over to the young teen.

"Hello, Louis." His is a voice that will become all-too-familiar to Louis throughout his life. "I'm Doctor Schofield. Jack that is, but my friends call me Jacky. Mind if I sit down?"

Louis raises his head; his eyes follow slowly in a foggy kind of way. "Are you a bloody psychiatrist?"

"Yes, Louis, I've been asked to talk to you." The man sits beside him.

"I ain't barmy!" Louis shouts, and the entire police station takes notice.

Doctor Schofield signals that it's okay and speaks even softer to Louis, "No one thinks you're crazy, son. They're just concerned, you know, because of what happened." He looks Louis in the eyes, "You want to tell me what happened?"

"Bugger off!" Louis lowers his chin into his chest and begins to cry, "It's all my fault."

Doctor Schofield drapes his arm over the boy and is caught off guard as Louis buries himself against the doctor's chest, crying uncontrollably.

"It's okay, son. We're going to get through this."

For the next ten days, Doctor Schofield meets with Louis twice a day, piecing together the events that led up to the night of his mother's death. By all accounts, Louis is a normal teenage boy. But Doctor Schofield does find certain events odd.

He stares down at his notebook. Keywords are circled. He starts deciphering his chicken-scratch handwriting. *Mother. Nurse. London. Father. Dead.*

He writes, *Mother was a nurse living in London. Met the boy's father, who died before the boy was born.* He makes a note, *Remember to ask how his father died.*

He checks his notes again. A small town north of London is circled as well as "sheep farm," "injection," and the word "disease." Ink flows from his pen as he composes the following sentence: *Mother moved to the small town* —he scribbles the name as he looks at his notes— *bought a sheep farm, lots of land,* then he writes in all capital letters, *THIS IS MOST DISTURBING.* He underlines the sentence a couple of times, *Mother used to lock Louis in a shelter at least once a month and would administer medication, which she told him was for his disease. Our lab results have come back negative for all known diseases.*

Doctor Schofield cups his chin in his hand, wrestling with the thought of why this would be.

A light flashes on the phone on his desk followed by the sound of his secretary's voice. "Doctor Schofield, Mr. Glover is here."

With a push of a button, he responds, starting a vocal tennis match. "Who?"

"Mr. Glover."

"And who is Mr. Glover?"

"The Kessler boy's guardian. He's here to take Louis home."

"Very well, Margaret. Show him in." He releases the button and quickly gathers his notes into a manila folder labeled with Louis's name.

A rather large, bald-headed, truck-driving type of man with a thick Lancashire dialect enters the room. "Mr. Schofield?" he asks.

"Doctor Schofield," he quickly corrects and gestures to the seat in front of his desk, "Yes. Please, Mr. Glover, have a seat."

"I'd rather just get the lad and be on my way." The man twists his wool hat within his hands.

"Please Mr. Glover, this will only take a moment." Schofield smiles a warm, reassuring smile, still extending his hand toward the chair, signifying that no matter how large and menacing the man may seem, he is not intimated and will not take no for an answer.

The man reluctantly sits. "Right, what's this all about?"

"Well, Mr. Glover." Jack takes a non-threatening posture, sensing a confrontational attitude. "I've been seeing Louis the past couple of weeks, and I'm just trying to piece some things together? Perhaps you can shed some light on some of them."

"I don't know how I can help."

"Did you know Louis's mother? I mean, did you know her well? You must have, if she's left her only son to your care."

He shrugs his shoulders. "Yeah, I guess? I mean, we weren't romantically together, but I would help her out whenever she needed it." His face grows red. "You know, with work around the farm. I didn't mean …"

"It's okay, Mr. Glover. I understand what you meant."

"It wasn't like that with me and her, she was a sweet woman, stitched me up a couple of times, saved me from going to hospital. Besides, I could never get a woman like that, real high society, but never made you feel like she was better than you. You know the type, Doc, really classy. Always smiling, always helping out people, never thinking of herself. I always told her she was stretching herself too thin. She took on too much, I always said."

"How do you mean?"

"That farm was too much, and trying to raise Louis all by herself."

Doctor Schofield opens the folder. "Do you know anything about Louis's father?" He searches his notes. "I can't seem to find out what happened to him and all Louis knows, is he died before he was born."

The large man fidgets in his seat, twisting his hat tighter and tighter.

"Please, Mr. Glover. It may help a great deal."

He takes a deep breath and sighs. "The boy's father was killed in London."

Jack raises his eyebrow, silently urging him to elaborate.

"There was an incident in Piccadilly Circus. The police were shooting at something and accidentally shot him. Louis's mother won a huge lawsuit; that's how she was able to buy the farm. Listen, I really have to get going. Can I get Louis now?"

"In a moment. You said she had her hands full with Louis. Do you think Louis is a handful?"

"He has his moments." Glover looks away. "You know how teenagers can be?"

"I'm afraid Louis ..." Schofield pauses. "I don't normally discuss a patient, but seeing how you're going to be the boy's guardian, I think you should know ... Louis believes he's seeing his mother."

"He's what?"

"Louis has told me that his mother has been coming to him. Telling him strange stories about his father and what he really is."

A perplexed look crosses the rough man's face. "And what does he think he is?"

"Something preposterous. Did you know Louis's mother used to lock him in a shed and use narcotics on him?"

The enormous man rises like a towering mountain, and for the first time, Doctor Schofield feels threatened. "Look, I answered all your questions! I just want to get Louis and go!"

"Okay, okay, Mr. Glover." Jack tries his best to calm the agitated man. "Certainly." He presses the call button. "Margaret, could you have Louis come to my office. And make sure he has everything he needs. He'll be going home with Mr. Glover." He looks into the large man's eyes as if to say, *Happy?*

"Thank you," the man breathes out, and already the doctor feels the level of stress dissipate within the room.

"I would like to continue seeing Louis, Mr. Glover. I think I'm helping him, and I do believe the boy needs someone to talk to."

"Yeah, well ... we'll see. It's really up to Louis now, isn't it? In a couple of years, he'll be a man, and I won't have a say in anything he does."

"He's going to need you."

"In more ways than you know, Doc."

Before Jack can ask what that last sentence means, Louis knocks on the door and enters. "Mr. Glover! What are you doing here?"

"I'm here to take you home, Louis," he says, arms hanging by his sides.

Louis runs and hugs the large man, who looks dumbfounded, like a man who's just reluctantly adopted a stray puppy.

Doctor Schofield silently motions for him to embrace the youth. Gradually, two arms the size of tree trunks wrap around the boy.

"Come on, Louis. Let's get you home."

Chapter 20
Late Night Dinner

Louis arrives at Jenny's door promptly at five o'clock with flowers in hand. She opens the door with an apprehensive smile.

"I hope I'm not too early?" he says handing her the flowers.

"No, it's perfect, and these are beautiful." She looks around the small apartment. "You want to come in?" She sweeps her arm in a large arc, poking fun at the tight quarters. "Welcome to my humble abode."

Louis steps past her, sensing an underlying tension.

"Well, this is a first; actually two firsts tonight," she says, bending down to retrieve a vase from beneath the sink. Louis looks inquisitive; his head tilts to the side. She frees the flowers from the clear cellophane wrapper and arranges them as water flows from the kitchen faucet, filling the glass vase. "Sure," she says, turning and placing the flowers on the counter. "The first time you're in my place, and the first time, I think, anyone in this town is going to see you after sundown."

Louis smirks. “I’m more of a homebody.” He moves closer. “And hopefully, this won’t be the last time you invite me to your place.”

She awkwardly sidesteps his advance. “We should get going. I was thinking we can go to the tavern. If that’s okay with you?”

He shrugs. “I was thinking of something a little more … upscale for our first date, but I’m fine with wherever you want to go.”

“It’s probably going to be packed.”

Confused, Louis counters, “It’s Thursday. Do a lot of people go out on Thursdays?”

Jenny makes her way to the door, this time sidestepping his question as she grabs her coat off a hook. “You want to take my truck or yours?”

Louis fumbles with his keys, making his way to the door, bewildered. “We can walk. It’s not that far.”

“Walk it? Are you—” She starts to say “crazy,” but quickly changes tack. “I’d rather drive, you know, just in case.”

“In case of … ?” he asks, having no idea what she’s talking about.

Jenny curls her fingers and snarls at Louis playfully, pretending to bite him around the neck. For the first time tonight, she’s warmed up to him in a manner he was expecting when he first arrived.

“For the love of … I guess I’ll drive,” he says, waiting for her to lock up. “You know, I would protect you.”

“How fast can you run?” she asks.

“How fast? Are you going to race me to the tavern?”

“Two guys come upon a bear in the woods,” she says, making her way to his truck. “The first guy whispers, ‘on the count of three we both run’ …” She looks at him and laughs. “The second guy says, ‘Are you crazy? Outrun a black bear?’”

He unlocks the door, and she slips inside, chuckling. "'I don't need to outrun the bear,' says the first guy. 'I just have to outrun *YOU!*'" She laughs as he closes the door and walks around the truck. He gets in as her laughter winds down. "You get it? I just have to outrun *you!*" She smiles. "So you see, Louis, I don't need you to protect me. I just have to be able to outrun you!" She continues to laugh harder.

Jenny is still laughing by the time the Land Rover comes to rest in the hardware store's parking lot. Louis beams with pride as Jenny exits the truck and takes his arm. Just as she predicted, the tavern is packed. *Everyone in town must be here,* he thinks. He focuses his eyes upon her as if trying to send her a question with his mind.

"I told you," she says, making her way through the packed dining room, "I think I see a spot in the back."

All eyes follow Louis as he trails Jenny. People break from their idle chit chat and study the flatlander. They find a small table for two, recently vacated, and sit, delighted to find a place. As the sea of people shift, a five-pointed star recently added to the tavern's décor comes into view. The freshly painted red pentagram is flanked by two burning candles on each side. Their wax drips, leaving long rope-like strands cascading down from their resting pedestals. Quivering black smoke trails from small flickering flames leaving hints of soot on the wall.

Louis's jaw locks when he sees it. He points and asks Jenny loud enough to be heard over the background noise of the bar, "Is that a—"

"Yeah!" Jenny yells back before he can finish.

"A pentagram! Really?"

"Yeah, I told you, Louis, the whole town is on edge."

"On edge is one thing, but that's taking things in a whole new direction! Is this why everyone is here?"

"Yes! Louis, No one wants to be home at night. Safety in numbers, right?"

"It looks like a scene from that movie in the eighties."

Jenny shrugs.

"This is insane. They can't really think that thing is a Wer—"

Taylor Jade drops a metal serving tray on the table and collects the empty beer glasses left there by previous patrons, interrupting Louis mid-sentence.

"Hi, T.J. When you get a chance, can we get two menus?"

Taylor's normal, innocent angelic disposition is hardened and she stares at Louis as if he ran over her cat. "There's no food for you here."

Jenny looks around. Every table has food on it and the entire bar is staring at them. "What are you talking about? What's going on?"

"I said, there's no food or drink for you here." Taylor Jade never takes her eyes off Louis. The entire place goes quiet. The bartender leans forward, his impressive chest like a cinderblock wall.

Jenny's jaw clenches as she prepares for a battle, but Louis stands and offers his hand to her. "Come on, Jenny. Let's go."

"No, wait—" Jenny starts, but Louis gives her a look and she concedes. The crowd parts as they head to the door.

Louis suddenly stops and bends over, clenching his stomach. The entire bar gasps and watches in horror as Louis throws his head back and starts shaking. He grabs his head and howls in pain. "Oh my God, Jenny, run!" he screams. She turns her back to him but before she can escape he grabs her by the waist and pulls her into him. "It's too late, Jenny!" He bares his teeth and throws his head toward her. A woman in the bar screams and the crowd recoils in terror. Her expression reveals fright as his immense body engulfs her tiny frame. His mouth cups her neck. A scream builds as she prepares for her throat to be ripped from her neck. Instead, tiny kisses move down her neck and her shock turns to warm, pleasurable surprise.

Louis's laughter starts down deep and bubbles over until it breaks into all-out hysteria. Jenny does not know whether to laugh or slap him.

Then Louis whispers, "Bear! I just have to outrun you!" And Jenny sprints to the door, giggling with Louis jogging close on her heels. Before the door closes, Louis yells into the bar, "Really, people? Monsters? This isn't some movie from 1981. It's the twenty-first-century!"

Louis is still laughing when they reach the truck. "Why don't we head into Windham and see what's open?"

Jenny nods and gets into the Land Rover. "Just need to outrun you; pretty funny."

Louis navigates his truck along the winding roads of Route 23, heading toward the popular ski town. Jenny chuckles every couple of minutes and then says, "That was brilliant! Did you see Mrs. Romano's face? And Mr. Brennan, I thought he was going to have a heart attack."

"I thought I was going to get shot!" He laughs. "They might have mounted my head over the bar right next to that eight-point buck. I shouldn't have done that." He looks at her. "I really shouldn't have done that!"

The sun was down behind the mountains. Only slivers of light broke through between gaps and valleys, lighting the tops of trees and the sides of west-facing mountains.

"I'm glad I can make you laugh," Louis says. "I was afraid when I picked you up I had offended you in some way."

Jenny gets quiet and then confesses. "It's not anything you did. It's what I've heard."

Louis waits.

Jenny points to the Chicken Run Restaurant. "They have great ribs. And I picture you as a *Cowboy Steak* kind of guy."

"A what?"

"A Cowboy Steak two-pounds of USDA Prime aged rib-eye beef," she recites as if reading it off the menu.

"Two-pounds! How much does that cost?"

"About eighty-dollars."

"Eighty-dollars! Blimey! That better be on hell of a steak! Does it come with mash potatoes?

She smiles. "Actually, they're really reasonable; it's just the Cowboy Steak that's expensive. And the food is fantastic."

"Why don't I just keep driving until you tell me what you've heard about me and then we'll decide on a place."

After several quiet seconds, Jenny breaks the silence. "Pete told me—" She wonders if it's a mistake to bring this up, but then a nagging feeling forces her to continue. "He told me you were in an institution."

Louis nods faintly, and softly says, "So I guess he told you about my mother."

Over a bottle of red wine, and a plate of *The Millrock's famous, Wonderfully Wicked Seafood Lover,* Louis chronicles his life, from the death of his mother up to the time he walked into the liquor store and first set eyes upon Jenny.

"So, it was a wolf, or wolves, that killed your mother?"

"That's what the official report said. They must have come around for the sheep, and when Mum went out there, even with the gun, they attacked."

Jenny's mournful expression shows heartfelt sorrow as a tear runs down her cheek. "And then that poor doctor. I never knew sheepdogs were so protective."

"He was like a father." Louis smiles, but Jenny can see the pain behind his eyes. "I never knew my father, but after my mother died, he was the first man in my life that actually cared about what I had to say."

Louis's head hangs low as he stares into a plate of leftover mussels and linguine. "He came to the village every Monday and we would talk. He always wanted to know how I was doing, and I never really asked him about his life."

Then Jenny sees his gaze grow despondent. "I loved that dog. I guess he must have thought the Doc was going to hurt the sheep. Before anyone knew what happened, Bosco lunged and caught him right in the neck. Doc was gone before the ambulance ever reached the farm. I had to put Bosco down right there with the police watching."

Jenny touches his hand, and Louis does his best to pull himself together.

"That was the main reason why I left England, just too many terrible memories. I thought I could make a quieter, simpler life for myself here."

"And now this thing happened with Oren. Oh, Louis, it must

have brought back so many memories."

Louis takes a deep breath and composes himself. "Well, there you have it, the life and times of Louis Kessler."

As if on cue, a server appears beside the couple. "Can I interest you in dessert? We have Flourless Chocolate Torte, or homemade Pumpkin Cheesecake, or perhaps something lighter like, one of our gelatos?"

"I think just the check." He looks at Jenny, who's nodding.

"Should I wrap this up?"

Jenny nods more aggressively. "I think that's a yes, my good man," Louis says. "I think the lady really enjoyed it. Everything was brilliant, thank you."

"I'll tell the chef," the server says as he makes his way to the kitchen with their leftovers.

"And you thought I was a meat-eater?" Louis jokes with a smile.

"Hey, little swimmy things are meat too."

The server places a white paper bag on the table, along with the check.

Louis surveys the damage, and then slips two bills in the envelope and hands it to their server. "We better get you home. It's quite late and I wouldn't want—"

"Shut up, Louis," she says, getting up as the server smiles at the generous tip. "I promise I won't ask you any more personal questions … tonight."

They walk to the door. "You can ask me anything, and I like that it's personal. It means we're connecting on a deeper level."

She slips her arm around his waist. "Slow down there, cowboy. Just because you bought me a dinner doesn't mean there's going to be any connecting, no matter how deep."

Forty-five minutes later, Louis and Jenny are lying on her bed, panting and naked. "I thought you said—" he starts.

"Shut up, Louis, and kiss me."

Chapter 21

Twenty-Four Years Earlier

One Fatal Mistake

The poor suspension and worn seats of the aging truck groan and bounce a young Louis Kessler with every dip and hole in the country road. The headlights flicker, cutting through the ever-growing darkness that seems to engulf the clunking truck as they make their way back to the small village. Louis keeps the window down despite the chilly night air freezing the side of his face. The potent scents of machine oil mixed with petrol fumes seep up through the floorboards.

"You're gonna stay with me." His large surrogate parent wrestles with the outdated truck's steering wheel. "At least for the next two years. Until you become of age, when you're legally able to be on your own."

Louis sits quietly.

Glover continues, "Louis, there are things you need to know."

Louis looks out the window. Between him and the endless

stream of trees passing by, unseen by the truck's gruff operator, sits the bloody, dead body of Louis's mother. Louis squeezes his eyes shut, shakes his head, rocks back and forth.

"I know you don't want to talk about things right now, Louis, but time is short and we're running out of it quickly."

In the darkness of this world, Louis is safe in the truck, and refuses to trust his eyes. Somewhere in his mind, he must be fabricating this hallucination. *Just go away, just go away, you're not real, you're not real,* he repeats in his head like a mantra. His foot rapidly taps the floorboard uncontrollably.

Listen to him, Louis, his mother's loving voice invades the darkness.

He opens his eyes and looks at the man who is taking him home. The once loving, warm hand of his mother reaches out and rests upon his knee. A cold, not-quite-icy sensation falls upon him. Not only his eyes, but his ears and touch now betray Louis. Doctor Schofield has said grief is a powerful thing, but Louis believes he might actually be going mad. *It's just the wind from the open window,* he lies to himself.

"Louis, do you know why your Mum locked you in the woodshed?"

For the first time since they've left the hospital, Louis speaks. "She said it was for my protection."

"Aye, in a way, yes," the big man agrees. "And did your mother always give you a sedative?"

Louis nods. "It's for my illness."

It was for the pain, she adds.

Louis chooses not to acknowledge his phantom mother.

"Your mother thought it would help the pain," Glover reinforces the dead woman's words.

"Doctor Schofield said I don't have any disease," Louis protests.

The big man nods his head. "How do I tell you this, Louis?" He sits quietly, with his lips curled inward, contemplating the words. Louis waits in anticipation. Finally, Glover speaks. "Your father came to the village one night." He turns and it's as if he's looking directly into Louis's soul. "And I cursed the day he came, him and that friend of his."

"What did they do? Kill someone?" Louis asks.

"No one asked them to come! No one wanted them there!" He continues, not acknowledging Louis's question. "Any other time would have been okay, but they came on *that* night. Why did it have to be that night?" He shakes his head as if it all happened yesterday, and then continues. "Your father and his friend were backpacking England. They came to the pub that night, just seeking shelter from the cold. They were like two frightened little lambs, they were."

Louis can see the large man's eyes tearing up with regret.

"We sent them away." He turns to Louis, searching for forgiveness. "All they wanted was a place to get warm and have some food, and we sent them to their deaths." His voice cracks as he speaks. He turns his gaze back to the road. "By the time we reached them, the one boy was dead and your father lay there bleeding."

Louis's mouth falls open.

The large man just shakes his head and keeps muttering to himself. "We should have never sent them away," he says, as if repeating it will turn back time and change the outcome. They sit quietly as the truck cuts through the darkness.

Glover slows the truck and it comes to a jerking stop outside his humble cottage. "We'll swing by your place tomorrow and pick up whatever you may need. But for now, it's late; let's get some food in you and get some proper rest."

The cottage is sister to the truck, with its unkempt appearance and neglected state. The strong pub-like aroma inside violates Louis's nostrils; the stench of sheep and spilled Guinness lays on Glover like an old worn-out bathrobe.

"There's a room in the back. It has a bed," the tall man says, hanging his cap on its customary hook by the door. "I'll have to clean it out tomorrow, but for now just move the junk to the floor."

Louis grimaces and an overwhelming sense of despair envelops him, darker than the corridor that leads to his unwanted domicile.

"Are you hungry? I can make you something."

Louis shakes his head. Somehow cooking is the last thing Louis can picture this man doing.

"You're probably tired? Need to rest, aye?"

A nagging question has been eating at Louis since he's heard the words uttered from his mother's appointed caretaker. "What did you mean, you sent them to their deaths?"

Sean throws a handful of kindling into the blackened cast-iron stove. Smoldering embers glow bright and devour the wood. Flames dance and he feeds a log to the hungry fire and quickly closes the heavy door, taking care not to burn his hand.

"You said you sent them out in the cold to their deaths. What did you mean by that?" Louis stands like David facing down Goliath. The large man shakes the cold from his coat and moves to the door to reacquaint it on a hook with his cap.

"It was a terrible night." He peers out the window. A whistle of wind rattles the pane. "Most of the town were gathered in the pub. We always gathered in the pub back then, on nights such as that one."

"And then my father came in?"

The large man nods, "Him and his friend, the little one." He starts shaking his head again as he did back in the car. The memories are stronger. He moves to the kitchen and pours a pint. Not waiting for the amber foam to settle, he brings the glass to his lips and consumes half of the thick, dark ale before continuing.

"It was that little one with his mouth." He tips the glass again, downing the rest of the stout, "I remember, I had just told a joke. About a Mexican and the Alamo." His memories show only in his own head. He stands there, a blank look on his face, as if he's watching a movie playing on the big screen. A smile pulls at the corner of his cheeks, then he bursts out a hearty laugh, *and he chucks the Mexican out of the plane!* He laughs for several seconds before growing quiet. "That's when the little fella asked the question. We were okay, up until then. Might even have let them stay, but something told us" —he stops himself— "something told *me* that little guy wasn't going to let it go!"

"Wouldn't let *what* go?" Louis asks.

"He asked about something painted on the wall of the pub."

"What?"

"Nothing! It's not important now. But I could tell …" He shakes his finger at Louis. "I could tell he wasn't going to let it go … and it was none of their business!"

"So you sent them away? Into the freezing cold?"

"NO ONE WANTED THEM THERE!" Sean slams the glass down.

"All they wanted was some food and to get warm!"

"They would have been fine if they'd stayed on the road." He pours another pint of Guinness and holds it in front of his lips, like an alcoholic momentarily contemplating sobriety. "If they'd just stayed on the road," he breathes out, surrendering to his demons and quenching his guilt.

After some time, Louis asks, “So what killed them?”

Chapter 22
A Troubled Childhood

Jenny rests on her elbows, twisting her chestnut brown hair around her finger, inspecting for split ends. As slow as a glacier, her lips curl into a smile. She closes her eyes and rests her chin against the crook of her shoulder. Louis watches her doelike eyes reopen. With one brow raised she asks, “I hope you’re not expecting me to make you breakfast, are you?”

Louis stretches, kissing her shoulder, pausing to breathe deeply of her scent. He closes his eyes, never wanting another moment to pass.

She runs her palm down her side and caresses her ass. The heat from the redness of tender slaps delivered in the throes of passion warms her fingers.

“I like the way you” —she pauses as the radiance warms her palm— “How do you Brits say it, ‘shag’?” She lets out a coquettish giggle. “There’s something primal about it.”

“I hope I wasn’t too rough.”

She drags her nails lightly down his spine. "It's the one time when people can act like animals."

She tenderly bites his shoulder. She moves on top of him. Louis feels her body warm his back. "Do you know, when lions mate, the lionesses are often seen biting the males." She clamps her jaw down on the back of his neck and growls.

"Okay, okay. I'll make breakfast," Louis says. "No biting."

She laughs in triumph, slapping his ass and rolling off him, sinking back into the bed. "You big baby. Don't like it when the shoe is on the other foot, do you?"

"Just tell me where the coffee is," he says, putting on his pants and pulling his shirt over his head.

"It's one of those k-cup things, right there on the counter next to the microwave." She bunches up the covers, rocking to find just the right spot. "I'll take French vanilla; I'm feeling Parisian," she says with a playful, catlike purr.

"Oh! And I got English Breakfast tea for you," she adds.

English tea in a small plastic pod. Bloody hell. Mum would be turning in her grave, he thinks and quickly adds, *if she was in her grave.* "One day I'm going to make you a proper cup of tea." He starts for the kitchen but yells back, "And just how did you know I would be having breakfast here?"

She grins, as only a girl who knows her true power grins. "Just a guess."

"You could have guessed a plate of scones or crumpets along with that English tea." Louis takes the milk out of the refrigerator after fumbling with the machine.

"Hello, Louis," the familiar voice calls from the living room.

Louis's head falls to his chest as his lungs deflate. *Christ, not now.*

"Is now a bad time?"

"Don't you have anything better to do? Please tell me you haven't been watching."

"Actually, no ... on both accounts." He joins Louis in the kitchen. The once human form bends and mimics the act of smelling the coffee as the final stream drips to the cup. "Oh, how I miss the smell of coffee."

"Get away from that." Louis pushes the once live Doctor Schofield aside and ejects the cartridge, replacing it with an Earl Gray cartridge.

"French Vanilla! I would kill for a French vanilla latte from Morty & Bob's in Kings Cross. Oh! And their grilled cheese! It's sublime!"

"I'm sure this is nowhere near the culinary experience of Morty and Bob's," Louis says, holding up the coffee mug, looking around for his uninvited guest. Instead he sees Jenny run to the bathroom, holding her hand to her mouth.

"You okay?" Louis shouts.

After several seconds she pops her head out. "Something I ate last night didn't agree with me." She wipes her lips with a bath towel. "I don't know who Morty or Bob is, but that smells delicious. I'm just gonna jump into the shower. Give it time to cool; I'll be right out."

"I just have to make a quick call," Louis says, and Jenny nods before closing the bathroom door.

When he turns around, the presence who used to be his therapist has rejoined the world of the living, sitting at the table holding the cup and saucer as if he's having High Tea with the queen. "Put that down!" Louis orders, then joins him at the table. "What do you want?"

"Remember how I just said I would kill for a cup of coffee? That's why I'm here."

"Not this again! I told you, I'm not killing myself!"

"I know you already took steps back in New York, The Last Will and Testament of Louis Kessler …"

"So, I had my will revised. Jenny has nothing. She could use the money." Louis bows his head. " I have no one else to leave it to. No family, no friends, no—"

"Cousins? I especially loved that story about getting drunk with yours. Where did that one come from?"

"A chap in a pub on Long Island told me that one. Look! It doesn't mean I'm swallowing a bullet anytime soon. It's just in case something happens."

"It's an awful lot of money, Louis."

"Certainly will change her life."

"Is that what you want to do … change her life?"

"I finally found someone who cares about me. And I care about her."

"Care about her? If you cared about *her* you would walk away, mate. Please, Louis, at least tell her the truth! A sheepdog? Really, Louis!"

"Tell her the truth? I tried that with you … and look how well that turned out!"

"I was foolish, Louis,"

"No! You were normal. It was a normal reaction to a not-so-normal confession!" Louis gets up, pacing around the room. "One I will not make again."

"Do I *have* to remind you of what you did?"

Louis stops in his tracks. "Don't you dare."

"So you're the one," a new voice mutters from behind Louis.

"You bastard," Louis whispers with eyes closed tight.

Dragging his half-torn carcass across the living room floor with his one remaining arm, Oren Goodman's mangled torso leaves a trail of shiny blood, like a slug oozing slime. The back of his head is torn open as clumps of gray matter slide down his back.

"I'm sorry, I'm so sorry," Louis repeats countless times. "I didn't mean for this to happen. I took precautions so this wouldn't happen!"

"But it did happen, Louis," his therapist says from the chair, banishing the hideous vision of Oren Goodman as quickly as it had appeared.

"This is why you have to kill yourself. It's happened before, and it will happen again. You'll kill Jenny."

"I would never hurt her. I love her."

"But you've already hurt someone you loved." The undead thing turns to the living room.

"Don't bring her into this."

"Louis, baby."

Louis falls to the floor and wraps his arms over his head. The sound of his mother's voice is more painful than the sight of Oren's misshapen corpse.

"You have to kill yourself, baby. You have to set us free."

"GO WAY. GO AWAY! GO AWAY!! GO AWAY!!!"

"Louis, is everything all right? Oh my God!" Jenny rushes over. Dropping to the floor, she tries to wrap her arms around Louis.

"GET AWAY! GET AWAY! YOU'RE DEAD! I WON'T KILL MYSELF! I WON'T!" Louis slides to the corner of the kitchen, his eyes still closed tightly.

"Louis, it's me! Jenny!" Kneeling on the floor, draped in only a towel with her wet hair matted to her back, she holds her arms out like some kind of patron saint of bathers.

Louis sits, knees drawn into his chest, like a child afraid to open his eyes from a nightmare.

Quietly she repeats, "Louis, it's me, Jenny."

He opens his left eye, then his right. "Is it really you? Are you real?"

His words baffle Jenny, and she sits back on her heels. “Of course it’s me. Who else would it be?”

Louis falls forward, landing in her arms. She holds him tight, feeling shivers move throughout his body. Louis takes a deep breath, wipes his eyes, and staggers to his feet. “I’m sorry, Jenny, I have to go.”

“I don’t understand,” she says, getting to her feet. “One minute you’re making breakfast and the next you’re on the floor yelling about killing yourself and asking me if I’m real? Just what the *fuck* is going on?”

“I have something ...” He searches for a lie and when none comes, he blurts out, “I have something I have to do.”

“You’re scaring me, Louis.”

Louis moves to the door.

“I’m going to come by after work, Louis. We need to talk about this.”

“NO!” Louis turns and marches toward her; his stern look scares her. He stops, realizing he is acting like a crazy man. “Jenny, look, you can’t come by tonight. Promise me!” He places his hands on her arms. “Promise me.”

“I’ll promise you, if you promise not to do anything stupid, Louis!”

“Stupid?”

“Like kill yourself!”

“Oh, no, you don’t have to worry about that,” he lies. “It’s just, I feel an episode is coming on, and I just have to go lie down.”

She looks at him with skepticism.

“I promise. I’m going straight home to take my medicine.”

“You’re taking medicine?”

Louis nods. “It helps in times like these.”

“Okay, Louis, but promise me we’ll talk tomorrow.”

“I promise.”

Chapter 23

Twenty-Four Years Earlier

You'll Think I'm Crazy

"Promise me." A younger Louis stands outside the shed. "Promise me you won't think I'm crazy."

"Louis," the familiar voice of his therapist reassures him. "Never would I think you're crazy."

"You thought I was crazy when I told you about seeing my mother."

"I didn't think you were crazy. It's a grieving process; quite a normal reaction to the death of a loved one. How have you been adjusting? Do you see her now?"

Louis looks toward his old house. His mother stands on the stoop watching him, a sad look on her once pretty, now mangled, blood-stained face. "No," he lies. His eyes dart to the ground, like an altar boy caught stealing. The doctor slowly glances toward the house, suspicious that there might be someone, or something, waiting there.

Louis moves inside the shed. The grassy smell of hay mixed with a musky aroma of farm animals lingers in the air like the tiny floating dust particles filtering through the slivers of light slanting across the dirt floor. Doctor Schofield follows. The shed's walls consist of layers of heavy wooden boards which are nailed one on top of the other, in some places five boards thick. At their weakest point, the walls are still one foot thick. Deep gashes are carved into the wood, as if some areas have been repeatedly slashed with an axe blade, or the claws of a gigantic bear.

"This is where your mother kept you?"

Louis nods. "To keep me safe."

"Safe from what?" Schofield runs his fingers over the splintered wood. "A battalion of England's Special Forces couldn't get through this. And you remember nothing of your time in here?"

Louis shakes his head, moving around the room like a former prisoner pacing his old cell. "I would come in here, Mum would give me a shot, and next thing I knew it was morning."

"Louis, I don't think you're barmy, but what your mother did—"

"What my mother did, Doctor, was protect this town and keep me safe."

Doctor Schofield recoils. "How so, Louis?

Louis retells the story that Sean Glover told him: how one night, two Americans came to the pub looking for shelter from the icy rain. Only they came on the wrong night, a dreadful night on which the townsfolk, —even though they knew it would turn deadly— sent them out into the moonlit night. He recounts how Sean and the other men in the town, overcome with guilt, went out looking for the two young Americans. How a man named Paddy

Talbot attacked the two on the moors. At least, that's the story they told police. By the time Sean and the others reached them, it was too late. The smaller one, as Sean referred to him, was already dead, but Louis's father lay bleeding, barely alive. Louis tells Schofield how Sean and the others covered up the story. Louis's mother, a nurse at the hospital, cared for his father until he was better. And how, even after he was warned of what he'd become, no one believed him. Just as Louis is trying to tell Doctor Schofield now what *he* is. He can see the skepticism in the Doctor's eyes.

"It drove my dad crazy. He tried killing himself, and still no one took him seriously!"

It takes over twenty minutes to tell the tale, and finally Louis ends with, "until Scotland Yard ended his life." Louis paces around the musty barnlike enclosure like a caged animal. The whole time, Doctor Schofield sits quietly.

Louis throws up his arms. "And now I suppose you'll tell me I'm barmy and it's all just a fantastic story to cover the fact that my mum was loony too."

"You said Sean told the police that a man named Talbot attacked your father and his friend, but that wasn't the truth?"

"It *was* Talbot, but not in his human form. Talbot was what is known as a lycanthrope."

"Louis, that *IS* crazy." The doctor stops himself, and quickly reassures Louis. "I don't think you're crazy, but I think what you've told me is crazy. There's no such things as wer—"

"Louis, what are you doing here?" Sean's overpowering voice cuts through the small dwelling. "Just what the bloody hell is going on here?"

Doctor Schofield gets to his feet. "Mr. Glover, Louis was just telling me about—"

"I don't care what the hell he was telling you." Glover kicks the heavy shed door, which swings back upon itself. The wood slaps the outside with a deafening *thwack*. "I want you gone!"

He points a sausage finger at Louis. "And you! You get back to the house."

Coming to Louis's defense, Schofield opens his mouth, but thinks twice as the large man stares him down and offers a friendly bit of advice. "Not a word from you, Doc or you yourself will be needing a doctor."

Schofield turns to Louis. "I'll be back, Louis. We'll talk more about this later."

"There'll be no more talk about this or anything else, Doc." He scowls at the passing physician. Louis stands next to him as he closes the dense wooden door and places a large, tree-trunk-sized barricade across it, locking it closed.

"Are you daft? You want to end up—"

"Shot down like a dog?" Louis snaps.

"I was going to say, *like your father!*"

Louis storms off toward the house, muttering under his breath, "Same thing."

Chapter 24
I Saw Your Boyfriend

The Land Rover's tires cross the double yellow line before darting back, kissing the white painted line of the shoulder. Gravel spits down the embankment and the rear end fish tails.

Down deep, part of Louis aspires to lose control and end up a highway fatality statistic. As he comes around the corner, two mountain bikers, hoping to get one last run in at Windham, swerve to avoid being hit.

The wheels bite the road, smearing ebony tire marks twenty feet behind the truck. Louis grips the steering wheel like a World War II Kamikaze fighter pilot who's had second thoughts, and struggles to pull his plane up from a dive. Regaining control, he holds a hand up apologetically, but both bikers throw him repugnant stares.

He brings the Land Rover back to a respectable speed and pulls in the parking field at Pratt's Rock. His hands tremble, partially because of the near homicides, but more because he'd heard his mother's voice in Jenny's apartment.

He summons his cynical therapist from his grave. "Why did you do that? We spent months talking about how fucked up I was over that."

"I'm sorry, Louis. But you have to realize, ending it is the only way."

"Maybe … maybe one day, but not today."

Officer Hanlon's cruiser heads South on Route 23, passing Pratt's Rock, the town's only claim to fame. He spots the sleek, Narvik-Black Land Rover in its parking area, and is curious. He flips on the lights and makes a U-turn. Officer Hanlon parks behind Louis's truck.

The electronic hum of the lowering driver's side window seems as out of place in the autumn countryside as Louis.

"Morning, Mr. Kessler. Lovely day."

"Good Morning, Officer Hanlon. Anything I can do for you? Or am I violating a town ordinance by sitting here?"

Pete looks up at the *Pratt Rock* sign and says, "New York's Mt. Rushmore."

"Excuse me?"

"I was just saying, our little monument here." He looks at Louis. "I mean, those aren't my words. Ripley called it that in his book *Ripley's Believe It or Not.* It's quite impressive, though. Are you heading up?"

Louis looks at the railroad tie stairs heading up to the information kiosk. "Up there? No."

"You really should. Zadock Pratt, had all these images chiseled into the rock up there. Quite breathtaking." Hanlon takes off his sunglasses, an attempt at intimidation. "So let me ask you: if you're not here hiking, what are you here for?"

Louis takes a deep breath. "Just composing my thoughts."

"Something upsetting you? Something you want to get off your chest? Maybe we should take a ride into town and discuss it back at the station?"

"If you must know, I'm breaking it off with Jenny before it gets too serious."

Officer Hanlon straightens. "Really?"

"Yeah, things just aren't working out. I figure in two days' time, you won't be seeing me around here anymore."

"Heading someplace warmer for the winter?"

"Something like that. I'm sure it will be warm where I'm going." Louis smiles darkly. "I mean, any place has to be warmer than here, am I right?"

Officer Pete smirks. "So, er … you leaving for good, or just for the winter?"

"It seems the majority want me to leave for good, so why disappoint them?"

"And what about your animals, the Scottish deer, you taken everything with you?"

Louis stares somewhere far out in front of him, "Every manner of beast is coming with me."

Pete taps the door. "Well, then. I guess, I'll say goodbye, Mr. Kessler. Make sure you leave a forwarding address, just in case there's further development in the Goodman case."

Louis nods and watches him return to his cruiser. The electronic sound of the rising window snugs the tinted glass back into place.

Moments later, Louis pulls into the town parking lot with eyes on Mountain Liquor. Throwing open the door, he heads straight for the counter. "Give me a bottle of Macallan."

Stacey, a somewhat aloof blonde, replies, "I don't think we have that."

"It's in the back."

She squints, wondering how he could possibly know that. "Jenny told me that's reserved for a special customer."

"I *am* that *special* customer!"

"I'll have to call her." She picks up the phone.

"Don't bother." He stomps over to the nearest shelf and grabs a bottle of Maker's Mark and a Bottle of Cutty Sark.

She rings him up, placing both bottles in a paper bag. "That will be—"

He throws fifty dollars on the counter and storms off.

"Hey! Don't you want your change?" Stacey yells to the closing door.

○☽☽☽●☾☾☾○

An hour later, the door to the liquor store flies open again. Jenny runs past the counter, making a direct run for the back room. Stacey's mouth opens but Jenny quickly throws a momentary "wait" finger her way as her other hand attempts to hold down last night's dinner.

The small store provides little shelter from the retching noises Jenny is making in the employee bathroom. All present stand motionless, their gazes fixed on either the floor or the label of the bottle they happen to be holding.

Jenny emerges, wiping her mouth with a paper towel. She stops, observing the patrons in the store. "Sorry, everyone." She smiles. "That's what you get for trying sushi at Al's gas station."

Some chuckle, a few laugh; everyone goes about their business.

"You okay, boss?" Stacey asks.

Jenny nods. "How's business been?"

"Not bad. That British guy came in asking for a bottle of Macallan. I said I had to call you —"

"Louis came in?"

"Yeah, kind of rude." She rings up a bottle of chardonnay. "Thirteen dollars, Miss Huhn."

"Did you sell him one?"

Stacey smiles, giving change. "Thank you, Miss Huhn, see you next Tuesday." *God bless her. Still drinking at her age.* Her eyes follow the silver-haired lady as she walks to the door, then she pivots to Jenny. "As I was saying, I told him I had to call you, because I didn't know he was ya' fella."

"Did you sell him one?" Jenny waits, raising her eyebrows and biting her lower lip, counting silently in her head to ten. *When I reach seven, I'm going to scream!*

"No. He got all bent out of shape and grabbed two different bottles of whiskey."

Jenny turns to the whiskey aisle.

"If you ask me, you could find someone nicer, like that sheriff fella. I think he's sweet on you? If I wasn't with Joey, I would hit that." Stacey cracks her chewing gum and raises her eyebrows, as if the thought of being with Officer Hanlon has already crossed her mind.

Jenny looks at her, as she's done a hundred times before. "It's officer, Officer Hanlon. Not Sheriff."

"I know. It just sounds better."

Jenny stares out the picture window down Main Street. *Going straight home to lie down, to take his medicine, my ass.* She shakes her head. *I have a good mind to go over there after work.*

Chapter 25

Twenty-Four Years Earlier

Doc, No!

A much younger Louis walks to the shed. Sean lifts the heavy, tree-like barrier and drops it to the ground. Louis breathes in the musty smell. *I can't believe I have to sleep in here.* He turns, clamps his hand down like an anchor on the door frame, "Do we really have to do this?" His eyes pleads, but Sean is stern.

"It's for my protection as well as yours." He tilts his head toward the lights of the town. "And theirs."

Louis peels his fingers from the pitted wood frame and slinks inside.

"I'll be back in the morning." Sean looks to the twilight. The burning heavens, as if painted in dying embers, await the rising moon. The heavy door thumps closed, the space becoming a prison cell as the securing brace snugs into the retaining brackets, cementing his sentence.

"This is crazy!" Louis screams, but his words are conveyed only as a muffled four-syllable shout to Sean's ears.

Glover hangs his head low. "I'm sorry, Louis, but I promised your mum," he murmurs as he leaves.

Driving from the hospital at not-quite-suppertime, Doctor Schofield decides to finish his conversation with Louis. *Maybe over dinner at the pub.* The country road is narrow and winding, but serene. The day's troubles recede into tomorrow's problems and Doctor Schofield is quite content watching the harvest moon rise over the moors. The warmth from the earth condenses in the cool night air, laying a blanket of mist close to the ground.

The doctor knocks on Sean Glover's front door with trepidation.

The door gives way to the larger, ill-tempered man. "What do you want?"

"Mr. Glover, I know this is a bit unorthodox, but I would like to speak with—"

"I thought I told you!—"

"Mr. Glover, legally I'm still Louis's doctor. Now you can either let me in or I can have the constable remove him from here and place him in my care."

A hand fit for a prizefighter covers a stubbled chin and strokes a granite jaw as Glover lets the words marinate. His lips pucker and then contort. "Yeah, well, he's not here. He's visiting my sister in Crickadarn, about a few miles southeast of Builth Wells." His other hand finds the edge of the door. "Looks like you came all the way out here for nothing. Cheers, Doc. Next time call first."

A strategically placed wingtip loafer impedes the door's closing. Glover's nostrils flare like a bull about to charge, his eyes focused on the shoe.

"You wouldn't be lying to me, would you, Mr. Glover?"

His eyes narrow, now focused deep within the therapist's eyes. "I don't take kindly to people calling me a liar, especially ones wearing girlie shoes."

"Then you wouldn't mind if I take a look around? You know, to make sure the boy is in a proper environment?"

The large man steps aside and lets the door swing open. "Help yourself, Doc."

Schofield sidesteps the big man. "Louis! Louis, are you in here?"

"I told you, Doc, he's not—"

"You didn't." The doctor's eyes search the man's rugged face as if reading a medical journal, until they find the answer.

"I didn't what?" the dumbfounded giant asks.

"You *did!*" Schofield hurries to the door. "He'd better not be in there!" He pushes the door open, making it crash upon the house's exterior. "Goddamn it, I thought his mother was bad. Has this whole town lost their minds?" Schofield runs to the car.

"Doc! Wait!" Glover runs to the fireplace and grabs the gun above the mantel. He runs outside, waving, the barrel of the gun an extension of his left arm. He makes eye contact just as Schofield pulls away. "Shit!" Glover jumps into the old pickup and pursues the doc into the darkness.

Schofield's car skids to a stop at Louis's old house. Glover's jalopy, only seconds behind, sputters as it comes to rest. The two men race to the field where the shed stands, Glover yelling, "Doc! Stop! He's not in there! Doc!!!!"

Schofield ignores the large man following close on his heels, but not close enough, as he reaches the large wooden brace. Glover digs his heels in, sliding to a stop and bringing the gun up. "Doc! Stop!"

Time stands still with Doctor Schofield's hands resting on the heavy wooden barricade.

His chest heaves up and down. "What are you going to do, shoot me? What kind of sick, twisted things have you done to the boy?"

"IT'S NOT LOUIS IN THERE!" The large man is truly terrified, only Jack is too blind to see it.

In one swift motion, Jack lifts the wooden brace and pitches it to the side. He swings the door open, hoping Glover won't pull the trigger. He is not prepared to see the horror waiting inside.

Only a small amount of moonlight falls on the floor in the otherwise dark room. Jack squints. Two yellow-green eyes stare back. He leans forward. "Lou—?"

Before the name can leave his lips, a fang catches him in the soft flesh below his jaw on the left side of his face. Another fang punctures the base of his skull on the other side of his head just below his ear. Before his mandible cracks and his carotid artery is torn from his neck, he feels a sharp sting in both arms as powerful claws grabs hold and pull him in. The pain is excruciating, but only for a brief moment, before Jack Schofield's lifeless body falls to the ground. The creature looms over its kill.

A single gunshot startles the beast, and it jumps back to the safety of its lair. Sean wastes no time closing the heavy wooden door. A fierce snarl shakes the walls. A stream of crimson flows toward the shed, feeding the blood lust, driving the beast mad. Sean fires another round and throws the gun into the braces, a temporary hold while he secures the timber across the doors. Clutching the gun safe within his hands again, Sean backs away slowly, keeping the gun barrel trained on the doors. At his feet, the body of Doctor Jack Schofield lays in the dirt.

Chapter 26
Three Not So Wise Men

The band of three—Bobby, Dave, and Joey—watch as Louis storms into the liquor store and comes out several minutes later. A plain brown paper bag shows the telltale bottle shapes everyone in town knows.

"Looks likes someone's going to tie one on tonight," Bobby says.

"I can't believe that limey bastard wouldn't let us hunt on his land," Joey frowns. "Pete said he's got these deer from Scotland, big as a moose. I bet he doesn't even hunt."

"Jimmy said he goes through an entire bottle each night and passes out cold till morning," Bobby replies.

Dave's eyes widen as if he has bigger game in mind. "I'll bet he knows what's killed Oren." He spits out a nasty wad of black sludge. "I bet he put up that fence just so that thing can run wild."

"I was talking to Vilma the other day at the diner. She said Pete walked Kessler's whole property. Even had John Guzzo's hunting dogs, but didn't find anything," Joey snaps.

"How'd he get on the Brit's property?" Bobby asks.

"He gave him the code. Vilma said Pete taped it to his computer so he wouldn't lose it in case he has to go back," Joey answers.

Dave pushes off the post where he's leaning and turns to Bobby. "Say, are you going into the station house to fix their crapper?"

"Yeah. I told Pete I would get to it by the end of the day, but I still have 15 minutes on my lunch hour before I head over there."

"I don't care about that," Dave says, moving closer as if to share a secret. "Pete has the security code for Kessler's main gate taped to his computer screen."

"You want me to fix Kessler's crapper?" Bobby asks, dumbfounded.

"No! Idiot. I want you to get the code when you go in to fix *their* toilet." Dave smiles. "Then tonight we'll do a little hunting for the thing that killed Oren."

He shakes his head, glaring at the Land Rover as Louis drives out of town. "I bet that piece of shit brought something up with him and set it loose to kill Oren."

The tiny lightbulb in Joey's head struggles to light, which makes him blurt out, "Gee, I don't know. I can't see him driving up from the city with a bear in the back of that truck. Wouldn't it tear up all that nice leather interior?"

"It's not like he drives it around like Zack's basset hound." Dave raises a hand but thinks twice about slapping Joey on the side of his head. *Maybe too many shots knocked the smarts right out of him.* "Did you ever think, *maybe* he brought it up in a cage when it was small. And now that it's grown up, it's too dangerous for him to handle? Either way, we'll take care of it tonight." He spits another disgusting wad of chewing tobacco as his eyes watch Louis's taillights disappear around the bend.

The sun is setting by the time the trio leave the tavern. The western sky is a scattering of blue with orange painted clouds, usually seen more in August than October. As the bright bursts of color fade, an inky blue veil descends upon the forest, turning the landscape black as tar. Somewhere in Dave's grownup heart, weathered by hard times and disappointment, he recalls a fond memory.

Since the age of twelve, Dave and Bobby have been hunting together (Joey joined them the following year, having missed the cutoff date to get his license). Ever since kindergarten the two boys have been like brothers, and since Bobby's father was never in the picture, Dave's dad raised him like a second son. So it only seemed right, when hunting season came around, that Dave's father schooled both boys on where to sit, what to watch out for, and of course, gun safety. The first time his dad took him hunting, Dave tossed and turned all night until his father cracked open his door at 5 a.m. and whispered the words he'd waited to hear. "Time to go."

Father and son had moved through the house as quiet as two church mice in Notre Dame Cathedral at midnight. Last-minute items were gathered and inventory was double-checked. Dave's father had that *don't-wake-your-mother* attitude, even though she'd been in the kitchen making them sandwiches and filling thermoses. The pre-dawn air had been cool, and it seemed as if all the rest of the world was safely nestled in their beds as they drove to pick up Bobby. Dave's father pulled the Dodge into the driveway and cut the headlights, hoping to avoid illuminating the interior of Bobby's small house. With just the running lights shining, both father and son saw what looked to be a tiny Elmer Fudd, wearing oversized orange vest and winter cap, sitting on the stoop. Bobby hadn't had anyone to make him sandwiches or fill a thermos of hot chocolate. No kiss goodbye or even someone to wish him luck.

"Morning, Bobby." Dave's father had spoken, sounding crotchety as the door creaked open like a screech owl calling into the nighttime air. Dave had grinned from ear to ear, happy to have his best friend with him for this first-time experience. This was the single finest memory of Dave's hunting expedition. Not his father telling him where to sit, or knowing his father trusted him with an instrument of death. Not listening to the forest come alive as he sat for hours without seeing anything. Not even accidentally squeezing the trigger to see if the safety was on, and hearing the thunder that came from the barrel, nearly blowing his foot off. Not the excitement on his father's face when he thought he'd shot a deer. All of those memories paled next to the one of him sitting in the truck with his best friend as his father drove through town while the rest of the world slept.

At the age of twelve, Dave and Bobby had seemed to have the entire world waiting for them. They were going to do great things. Every refrigerator cardboard box was a castle; every stream a vast river leading to new and exciting lands for them to explore. They dreamed of seeing the world, traveling to exotic places. Meeting women and—even though the thought of it was yucky—getting married and having kids of their own. Dave hoped to be the kind of father his dad was to him, maybe even better. But one thing had been for certain: one day he would take his own son hunting with him. He would show him where to sit, what to look for, and beam with pride when he brought down his first buck. And maybe, just maybe, there would be a best friend for his son to share that experience.

Dave sits serenely and drives, like his father had on that morning so many years ago, and smiles, feeling lucky he has such good friends.

As instructed, Joey stops at Oren Goodman's farm and picks up a small hog. Bobby was successful at fixing the bathroom at the police station as well as obtaining the security code that unlocks Louis's main gate. As the rusted Ford clambers down the country road with its three passengers crammed inside, Bobby asks, "What's the pig for?"

"Don't you know anything?" Dave sneers. "We're going to use it as bait. Unless you want to be tied to a post?"

Joey snickers. "Yeah, Bobby, don't worry, Dave and I will keep a sharp eye out. And when that big old grizzly comes down for a midnight snack," he laughs hard. "BAM! We'll nail him."

"Yeah," Dave adds. "We'll have his hide stuffed on display upstairs at Young's."

Dave parks the beat-up Dodge half a mile before Louis's gate in an old, seldom-used cut-off. Before he can reach for the handle, Bobby stops him. "Isn't he going to know it's us, when someone's opening his gate? I mean, usually those type of security things sound some kind of alarm."

"Relax, Bobby." Dave checks his watch; a little past 7 p.m. "From what Jimmy told us, and judging by how quick Kessler wanted to get those two bottles home, I'd say that alkie is probably three sheets to the wind by now."

Bobby sighs. "I got a bad feeling about this, Dave."

Chapter 27

Twenty-Four Years Earlier

Darkness Takes Hold

When you close your eyes, there is darkness. But you can still hear sounds all around you. You can still feel slight changes in the air as it caresses your skin, awakens the tiny hairs, raises goose bumps on your arms and the back of your neck. You can smell the rich, smoky roasted aroma of coffee brewing. Or the sweet smell of lavender as your lover draws close, anticipating the moment their soft, silky lips kiss yours.

But in the void of blackness right before you awake, emptiness prevails. And in that brief moment, before you stir, nothing exists. It is this state that a young Louis inhabits. No tingle of the legs, no twitch of the spine. No dreams of standing naked in classrooms … only darkness.

Until a familiar voice calls into the black pitch. "Louis."

The words are soft and low, barely arousing the spirit. "Louis, wake up."

Slowly, the blackness melts away into the tangible world, and the senses awaken. Eyelids instinctively flutter closed again, shielding against the invading light.

"Hello, Louis." A greeting Louis has come to know from his many weekly sessions with Doctor Schofield.

Louis tastes the gritty dust crusted to his lips and feels the hard, cold earth against his cheek. He is lying on the dirt floor of a wooden structure. Sunlight streams in from narrow gaps in the wood slats of the roof.

A voice coming from the darkest corner of the room ushers in a new day. "Louis, do you know where you are?"

Louis blinks several times, allowing his eyes to adjust. "I'm in the shed," his words shake.

"Good. And do you know why?"

"I told you why. You laughed and said I was barmy." Louis stops, realizing he's naked. He covers himself, wondering where his clothes are.

"I never said you were crazy." The darkness surrounds the doctor. "And do you know what you did last night?"

Louis looks around, trying to piece together last night's events.

"It's all true, Louis."

Louis finds his clothes and sheepishly gets dressed.

"What's the last thing you remember about last night, Louis?"

Louis faces the figure hiding in the shadows. "I remember walking around for the longest time. I was getting tired. I tried to lie down." His face contorts with all the puzzlement of a victim lost to Alzheimer's.

"It was hot!" He stops and looks down. "No! I was hot! That's when I ripped off my clothes." A spark of remembrance: "I was burning up, and then … and then the pain came." His expression is anguished. "Worst pain I ever felt! Like growing pains in my knees

… only all over my body."

"And then what, Louis?"

"And then … and then. I don't remember."

The figure in the corner shifts. "You don't remember me coming here?"

"You came here?" Louis searches his memory. "I can't remember anything from last night."

"I came here to save you." Schofield's voice grows stern. "To prove to you what Sean told you wasn't true. I opened the doors, Louis. And do you know what you did?" Doctor Jack Schofield steps from the shadows. The darkness gives way to a repulsive sight. His voice crescendos with rage. "You tore me apart!"

Streaks of sunlight fall on the half missing face of Louis's therapist. Louis recoils in horror. Dried rust-colored blood stains the front of the doctor's clothes. Flesh dangles from deep gashes torn down to the bone. Tears streak down Louis's face as Schofield approaches.

"And now, I'm to understand, I must stay in this state of limbo until the bloodline is severed." He grabs Louis and holds tight. "You have to kill yourself, Louis!"

Chapter 28
Who's Hunting Who?

With the successful retrieval of the code on Officer Hanlon's desk, and regardless of Bobby's feelings, Dave punches the seven-digit code into the keypad, granting access to Louis's property. Every horror movie has that pinnacle moment when the victims could have changed their fate if they just walked away. Bobby and Joey feel *this* could very well be *that* moment. Dave, not so much. And with determination, he walks through. The other two exchange looks and follow.

Behind them, a foreboding metallic clank relocks the gate, sealing their fate. Light from their three cellphones dances on the dirt road as the band of three tracks half a mile with the pig in tow. Dave takes a left off the road and heads through the brush toward a clearing he'd spotted earlier on a satellite image from Google Maps. Buried deep, somewhere in all of their terrorized brains, a line from an eighties movie warns, *Stay on the road, and beware the moon.*

When they get to the clearing, Dave ties the helpless pig to a small sapling pushing up from the grass. He rejoins the others and points to a rock wall at the northern perimeter. "Joey, I want you up there, and Bobby,"—he points to a thickly wooded area to the east—"I want you up there." He points over his shoulder. "I'll be across the meadow, this way, so no matter which direction this thing comes from, one of us will get a clean shot."

Dave starts across the grassy plain, trying to be as quiet as he can and in a low voice calls back, "Remember, the attack on Oren came at around one in the morning, so we may be in for a spell."

Joey checks the time on his cell phone, 7:20 p.m. *Great. Five hours sitting on a rock wall in late fall, freezing my ass off. I should have volunteered to be the one tied to the tree.*

Bobby watches as Dave disappears over the ridge and Joey takes his position upon the rock wall. *Sounded just like his dad.* A quiet resettles over the field as the moon crests over the eastern mountain range, bathing the nighttime sky in a velvety silk blue hue. Bobby pulls a small silver flask from his jacket and takes a swig. Resting his gun in the crook of his arm, he mats down the tall grass and flops on his ass. The weight of his years topples him backward, and he rocks like a tortoise till he achieves a sitting position. The meadow sleeps; even the hog beds down.

Joey rests his gun against the trunk of a large oak tree and pulls beer after beer from every pocket of his oversized winter jacket. He taps the top of a can with his fingernail, sending a tinny sound, like a metallic woodpecker, across the meadow. White foam sprays from the can and Joey gulps the suds along with half the can. He wraps the left flap of his jacket under the right and crosses his arms, cradling the beer in the bend of his arm. He cranes his neck as he bends backward, draining the rest of the beer down his gullet.

○◗◗◗●◖◖◖○

By the third beer, Joey is feeling the pressure. Nature is calling, as the townsfolk would say. He touches the screen of his phone and it lights up with what seems like a hundred candles. His pudgy fingers tap at the letters, missing their intended targets. *Thank god for auto-correct.* Across the field, two other cell phones vibrated to life.

"Anything?"

Moments later the responses came back.

"Nothing yet."

"All quiet here."

Joey thinks about cracking a fourth beer, but first, *better make some room.*

Testing each rock with his boot before placing his weight firmly down on solid footing, Joey climbs over the rock wall that separates the field from the forest. Staring into the dark woods where the moonlight is blocked by the canopy of trees, he can only make out shadowy shapes of trees and rocks. Occasionally the wind blows and the mighty pines rub together like timbers of a sailing ship, groaning and creaking.

Joey blows on his hands, warming them with his breath before unzipping his pants and feeling the icy air on his naked flesh. The warm liquid flows from him, creating rising steam in the crisp night air. He lets his head fall back, gazing at the night sky. Even with the light of the full moon, the Milky Way is clearly visible, stretching across the heavens. Joey searches for satellites as he often did as a boy, remembering his father pointing them out and wishing he had a son of his own to share that memory. Feeling his business is near completion, he moves his attention from the heavens back to earth.

Something peculiar catches his eye. Where before he could make out three rocks jutting out of the ground in the distance, now there are four. Then somewhere among those four rocks, a twig snaps. Joey stands motionless, still exposed. Despite the cold night air, a bead of sweat gathers at his temple until gravity pulled it down over his cheek. He slowly fumbles around his groin, uncertain which one of the newly added outcrops has materialized. He can feel his heartbeat rapping on the side of his neck.

As slowly as his hands move, one of the center rock rises, growing ever larger until it reaches the size of a man. The shape starts toward him and he can see the outline of arms hanging at its sides. Joey sighs heavily, pulling up his zipper. "Mr. Kessler, you scared the shit out of me."

Louis Kessler's looming silhouette silently edges closer.

"I know what you're thinking. We shouldn't be here and … and …" He gulps for air, flashing his best Humphrey Bogart smile. "…and you're right. That's on us. We're sorry."

Kessler stands twenty feet away. Joey sees the thick fur coat he's wearing and thinks, *I knew he was a dandy man, but he could have thrown on any old jacket to come down here to talk to us. How did he even know we were here?*

The monolithic figure stops. Now Joey can make out its large, triangular head mounted upon a hulking mass. The head moves and Joey catches two protruding ears perched on each side. *Not Kessler,* he realizes. The urine left in his bladder warms his cold leg and runs into his boot.

The creature drops to all fours as Joey staggers backward, tripping over the rock wall, falling on his ass, thrashing his feet, trying to find a foothold.

The beast moves forward cautiously. Intently. Calculating.

Joey falls down the side of the rock wall, landing on cold, damp grass. He has pulled his legs under him, moved to get up, when he sees a massive hand reach over the rock ridge and clamp down on the stone. Its razor-sharp claws scratch upon a teetering stone, which shifts under the creature's weight as it smashes the bracing rock. The massive creature seems to double in size, now close to its prey. Joey pushes off the ground with both feet, launching backward, five feet, but the creature is on him in one leap.

Ten knifelike claws pierce his body, pinning him to the ground as the weight of the creature crushes vital bones. Joey cries out with every ounce of breath left in his lungs: "ARGGGGG! DAVID! PLEASE HELP ME! PLEASE! DAVID! SHIT! HELP ME! OH, GOD!"

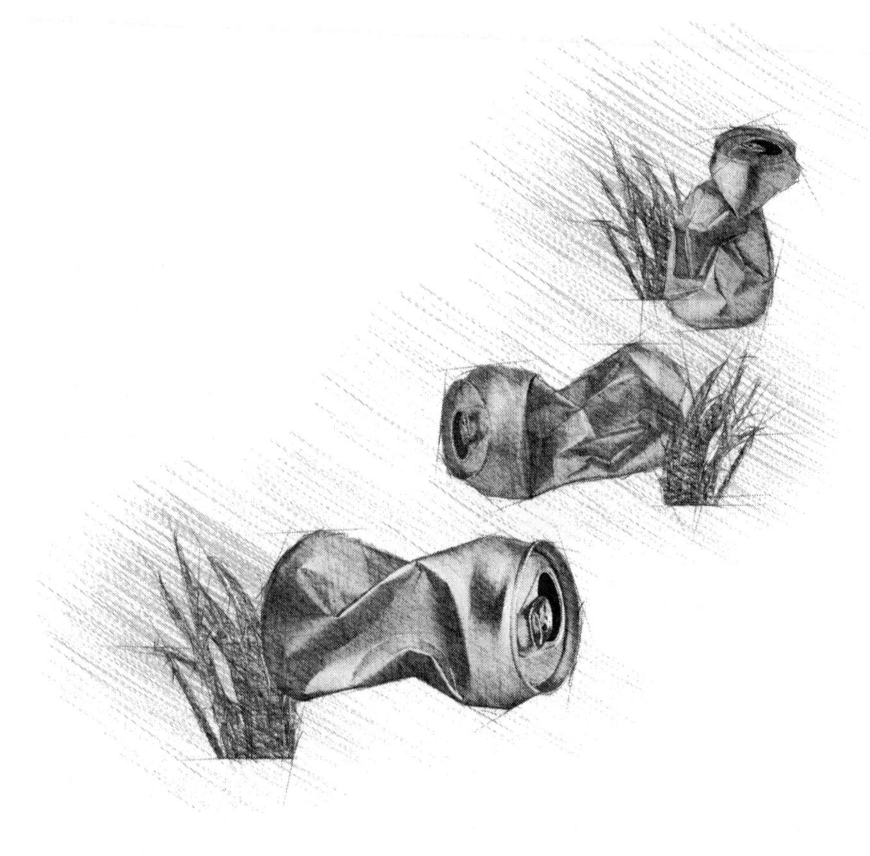

Chapter 29
Stop and Listen

Jenny watches the second hand of the clock above the store's door as it descends to the valley of the six. She sighs as it begins its ascent up to the peak of the twelve. Ten to eight. Ten minutes to go and not one customer for the last two hours. *God forbid I close nine minutes early; I'd never hear the end of it if old man Spano wants a nightcap and has to go to bed three sheets to the wind and not four.*

Like a high school student on the last day before the summer recess, Jenny's only focus is ticking away. The minute hand jerks forward, then seems to drop two minutes back. "Ah! Come on!" Jenny slams her hand down on the countertop. "That's it, I'm calling it! Time of death seven-fifty-three!"

She hurries to the front door, scans the parking lot. *Nothing moving.* She flips the plastic open sign to closed, hurries back, hits the cash register drawer open, and stuffs the day's profits into a green payroll bag, then zips it closed. In the back, she secures the bag in the safe. *I'll tally that tomorrow, I have a liar to deal with,* she decides.

Hitting the lights as she locks up, she checks her phone. *Eight o'clock on the dot.* "Ha, no late-night staggering home for you, old man Spano."

Firing up the Chevy, she sits impatiently, but lessons taught by her father don't die so easily. *Always warm up the engine, sweetheart, especially on a frigid night.*

But after a minute, she yanks the gearshift into drive. *Well, the night's not that cold,* she thinks.

The blinking traffic light paints the street yellow and red as it alternates, there between Main Street and the empty parking lot. *It's deader than twenty below on Christmas Eve, and I'm worried about leaving ten minutes early? What's going on?*

Jenny's question is soon answered as she approaches The Prattsville Tavern. The New York State Fair could not hold more people than are stuffed into the town's watering hole. People are lining the sidewalk outside, some carrying rifles slung over their shoulders. Every car, truck, and bicycle, which normally fill the grocery store's parking lot, are parked along Main Street or in the hardware store's parking area. Jenny slows as she passes, astonished by the crowd. Finding a parking spot halfway down to Moore's Motel & Resort, Jenny heads back toward the tavern.

The crowd inside resembles the front row at a Rolling Stones concert. Bouncing from elbow to shoulder, pushing forward and backward sometimes at the same time, Jenny feels like she's swimming in Jell-O. An opening in the sea of people allows her to find a friend. "Christine, what's going on?"

A slightly inebriated blonde hugs Jenny. "You made it! Let mee get you a drink." Jenny waves her off and repeats the question. "Oh," Christine says, "it'sss the firsth night of the ffull mooon." Her words are slurred but still somewhat coherent.

"What?" Jenny looks at the faces of her friends and neighbors.

People she grew up with and went to school with. Young and old. The bedrock of Prattsville, now corralled like sheep, huddling together, fearing a made-up Hollywood legend.

"I'm getting out of here," Jenny yells into her friend's ear. The girl smiles, her dreamy eyes lazily tracking a tall farmhand moving toward the bar. She's oblivious that Jenny is leaving.

Breaking free into the night, Jenny breathes her first breath of fresh air since being engulfed in that mass of rural America. She makes her way down the center of the abandoned street, feeling like the last sane person on earth. Two short horn bursts let her know she is not alone. Rolling up on her slowly, Pete rolls down the window and stops. "You must be the only one who's not in the tavern tonight."

"Hey Pete, I just came from there. It's a real sardine can. What's with the guys out front with guns?"

"Oh, they're alright. It's not as bad as hunting season. Anyway, if someone has to carry a gun to make themselves feel safe, not much of a man, I always say."

"Still, could be a fire hazard?"

"I'd rather have everyone in one place, makes my job easier." He chuckles and smiles. "I'll hang around, start breaking them up in a couple of hours. Hey, did you see Joey Porter in there? His wife called, said he didn't come home tonight."

Jenny shrugs. "It's so packed in there, he could have been right next to me and I wouldn't have seen him."

"Yeah, now that Nick's is closed down, the tavern's the only place people have to go." After a moment, he looks as if something else has suddenly occurred to him. "I haven't seen Bobby or Dave, either. I wonder if the three of them went into Windham. Maybe I'll take a ride down that way. Hey, where are you headed? Wanna take a ride?"

Jenny shakes her head. "Nah, thanks, I was just gonna drive …"

"You're not going to see *him*, are you?" Pete protests.

Jenny lawyers up, "I don't see how that's any of your business, sheriff."

"Jenny, please! I'm not buying any supernatural bullshit, but something killed Oren Goodman, and that something is still out there, probably in those woods." Officer Hanlon can see the gears turning inside her head. "At least for my sake, promise me you won't go out there tonight."

The words *"promise me"* strike a chord. Jenny did promise Louis she would not go up there tonight.

Pete continues. "It's not a jealous thing … I'll drive you up in the morning and gift wrap you to him, if that's what you want, but please, Jenny, I can't take responding to another call like that one." He looks deep into her eyes. "Not with you involved. It would break my heart. And it's not sheriff, I'm an officer."

"I know. It just sounds better." She smirks. But whether it is his words that sway her or her father's words reminding her, *When you make a promise, you make a bond that cannot be broken,* she nods and leans down, sliding her head through the open window. She delivers a soft kiss on the stubbled face of a man who's worked a long day. "Thank you, Pete. You don't have to worry, I'm heading home."

As Jenny heads to her car, Hanlon turns the cruiser around, bound for Windham. She stops and listens. The crowd outside the tavern stops and listens. Even Hanlon brakes, and listens. Reverberating in the distance, hidden somewhere in the mountains of the Catskills, an unearthly howl proclaims another kill.

Chapter 30
Finishing Dinner

The body of Joey Porter, or what's left of it, lays silent on the frosty ground. His still-warm internal organs send condensing vapors dancing into the autumn night air. Bobby and Dave race across the field, guns at the ready. Bobby is closest and stops short of the motionless mound of flesh that was only moments before his best friend. Dave runs past him, sliding to a stop. Looking down, he jumps back, fearing he is trampling on his friend. A terrorizing howl rouses them back to reality and both snap their guns into position, fanning the meadow and woods. Twenty yards into the woods, a tree branch snaps. They fire three thunderous shots in its direction, one from Dave and two from Bobby.

In a soft hunter's voice, Bobby asks, "Did we get it?"

The more experienced hunter stays quiet, listening to the forest. A long, deep-throated growl farther away confirms the contrary. Bobby looks at Dave, then down at the carcass that was his friend, then back to Dave. "What is THAT?"

Dave pans his rifle slowly, calculating movement and distance. He closes his left eye, sharpening his focus through the scope with his other. Muscles flex in his forearm. Ever so gently, he squeezes the cold, steel trigger. The reverberation from his .35 Remington echoes through the mountains, and instinctively, Dave chambers another round.

"You got it! You had to have gotten it!"

"Shut up, Bobby." Dave trains his eye through the scope, listening.

Suddenly there is a howl right where Bobby had been sitting. Bobby fires next, wildly, out of control. Another two rounds wasted in the dark. Now Dave can hear something cutting across the field just beyond the hedgerow.

"Jesus Christ, Dave, it's circling us!" Bobby cradles his gun in the crook of his elbow, and frantically unscrews the cap on his metal flask, throwing his head back as the bottom of the flask raises to the heavens. The thing is now making its way to the treeline to the north. Bobby drops the empty flask and follows Dave's movement with his gun. He glances over his shoulder to the hog tied in the field and thinks, *the only difference between that pig and us, is we're not tied to no tree.*

"Dave, let's get the fuck out of here," he whispers urgently.

"Easy, Bobby boy, I'm not leaving after what this fucker did to Jo—"

A long, dominating howl, louder than Dave's Remington, shakes the forest.

Bobby fires four more rounds, blanketing the area. "SHIT! I'm out." He pats his jacket and pants, searching for more bullets. "Let's go, Dave!"

Dave turns on Bobby like a madman possessed. "I told you,

I ain't going! Not without that thing strapped to the front of my truck!"

"What the fuck am I going to do! Throw a fucking stick at it! I'm as helpless as the pig out there." He throws his arm out, pointing in the direction of the hog.

Dave looks past Bobby to the edge of the rock wall. Bobby spins around, expecting to see the creature lunging at him. His foot slips, probably on an organ, or not yet congealed blood, sending him falling on his ass.

"What the hell! Why the hell are you scaring me like that?"

Dave nudges his chin toward an old oak tree growing up from the rock divider. Joey's Marlin .336 is leaning up against the trunk.

"Fuck NO!" Bobby lumbers to his feet. "If you think I'm going over there, you're out of your fucking mind!"

"Listen, Bobby, I don't know how many rounds I have left. You want to be standing here with your dick in your hands when that thing makes its stand?"

Bobby wrestles with his thoughts like a faithful husband wrestling with the idea of a hooker in Vegas.

"I'd feel a whole lot better if two guns were firing." Dave points the tip of his rifle toward the tree.

"Okay, okay. I'll go. But you better cover me, and I mean really well!"

"I always have, Bobby boy." Dave locks the Remington tight against his shoulder.

Bobby moves as slowly as a high schooler sneaking into a cemetery on Halloween. He stops and listens. Not a sound. No sound of the creature, or any creature. Nothing is moving in the forest. Never a good sign. He looks back at Dave, who is urging him forward. The autumn grass betrays his position with every step, crunching louder the closer he gets to the stone border. Six feet away and he feels the cold travel down his back. His heartbeat pounds against the side of his head. His breathing is fast, and all he can think about is pouring a bottle of whiskey down his throat when this is all over.

Four feet away, he sees three beer cans resting on the rock wall. Not brave enough to get the gun, but he's been known to fight bikers over a can of Coors Light.

Three feet away, and he can almost reach out and grab Joey's gun. One more step and he'll have it in his hand. His right foot lands and he hears the pig squeal. He twists at the waist, trying to get a look at the pig. In front of him, the sound of claws dig into tree bark. A low growl comes from behind the tree and Bobby realizes, *he is the pig.* He gives Dave one last *help me* look and turns back to face his nightmare.

Using its arm like a pivot, the creature swings from behind the oak. Its hindquarters dig into the base of the tree as its other arm comes sweeping around in a great arc. Its fingerlike claws catch Bobby just under the jawline, puncturing his carotid artery. Blood sprays high in the air, painting the rock wall a deep Pennsylvania-barn red. Before Dave can pull the trigger, Bobby's head is ripped from his body and is hurtled toward him. Dave screams in terror at the sight of Bobby's trusting eyes staring back at him as the head comes to rest right at his feet.

Dave's muscles will not respond. He knows that thing is twenty feet away and he should raise his rifle and fire, but he cannot move. The small twelve-year-old boy who sat on the stoop waiting for his first hunting trip is now looking up at him, still blaming Dave for not listening to him. His brain scrambles as he tries to process Bobby's head without his body. Dave's eyes are the only part of his body that moves as they break away from Bobby's gaze and move across the blood-trailed clearing to the oak tree. The creature sways, as if standing at the bow of a ship in calm seas. Blood falls from its mouth, matting the tufts of black fur upon its chest. Its yellow-green eyes transfix upon its next victim, waiting for the prey to make the first move.

Dave raises the rifle. The creature bears its sharp, blood-stained teeth. Dave halts this plan of attack. The small region of Dave's Neanderthal brain known as the hypothalamus activates the sympathetic nervous system, sending the fight-or-flight instinct through the autonomic nerves to the adrenal glands. The hormone epinephrine pumps from these glands, all sending the wrong signal to Dave's brain.

RUN!

Before his rifle even hits the ground, he is several yards away.

Now anyone who has a cat, or any predatory animal, knows that it will chase anything that runs. And that is exactly what the creature does.

Bobby Wilcox's headless corpse surrenders the last amount of blood as its final heartbeat pumps thick red ichor upon a bed of fallen leaves, and stops. Puddles of coagulating blood oozing from a stump of a neck. The beast leaps over the carcass, landing heavily between its first and second victims.

Dave hears the beast grunt as it lands. He prays for the first time in years. There is no God in the field tonight, however, and before he can get out the words *'please God—'* the beast's jaws lock onto the back of his head. Sharp, surgical needles pierce behind his ears and his skull cracks, his legs go limp, and the weight of the beast pushes him forward. Dirt fills his mouth and rocks bite into his cheeks and break his nose. The air in his lungs is forced out by the immense weight on top of him. His limbs flail out of control and he sees only black before being spun around to gaze up at the heavens. The beast rolls onto its back, cradling Dave to its chest. Strong hindquarters tuck under and kick in several rapid thrusts, much like a cat playing with a ball of yarn. Long claws from the creature's feet dig into Dave's lower half, throwing pieces of flesh and cloth ten feet behind him. Dave sucks in one last breath and exhales a scream of pure phantasmagoria. Jaws crush the annoying sound and the field is quiet once again.

The pig lies peacefully under the light of the harvest moon.

Chapter 31

Twenty-Four Years Earlier

Promise Made

"Kill myself?" The words barely register as a younger Louis Kessler stands mortified watching his therapist's mangled, half-missing mouth try to form the words.

"Louis, look around you. Your mother locked you in this cell for sixteen years of your life."

Louis looks at the thick, clawed panels of wood. His thoughts return to the corpse talking to him. "Doesn't that hurt?" He points to the open flesh wound, exposing the doctor's windpipe.

"It did. It doesn't anymore. I feel nothing."

"Shouldn't we get you to hospital?"

The doc walks to the barricaded door. "Louis, my body is lying right outside."

"Then shouldn't we call someone, do something?"

"Everything has been done. Sean is seeing to that." He turns to Louis. "Now, I need you to listen carefully …"

Louis makes a grotesque face, trying not to stare at the macabre figure he's created.

"Your father was attacked by a lycanthrope, a lightning-back. He survived, and because of that, he became one."

"But I wasn't. I didn't even know my father."

"It doesn't matter, Louis. His blood flows through your veins. Part of his genetic makeup made you, and because the lycanthrope gene was part of that makeup …"

"I'm one too." Louis shakes his head. "And my mother knew this?"

From the corner of the room, a loving female voice answers, "Yes, Louis."

"Ahhhh!" Louis jumps as the phantom, who was once his mother, walks closer. He spins, throwing his hands up, addressing his therapist. "You told me she wasn't real! You said I manifested her to cope with her death!"

"Louis." His mother's sweet voice beckons from beyond the grave. "Anyone you kill is forever trapped in a place not of this world, unable to move on."

"BUT I DIDN'T KILL ANYONE!" he cries, falling to the floor, tears streaming down his face.

"You didn't, but the thing you become has," Jack explains.

"Oh, honey. I know you would never do anything like this, but that other part of you, the beast you become, it can't help it … all it wants to do is kill." She places her hand upon his shoulder.

Louis throws his arms around his mother, sobbing uncontrollably. "I don't want to die."

The corpse that once was a beautiful woman looks up at Jack with pleading eyes.

Softly, he concedes. "Louis, if you *promise* never to kill. If you can prevent this from happening *ever again*, I guess your mother and I can wait until nature takes its course, and you die from natural causes."

She strokes his hair. "I've watched over you for sixteen years. Now that you know what you are, and with Sean's help, what happened to me and Dr. Schofield should never happen again."

Louis sniffles and wipes his eyes. "I promise, I PROMISE! I never wanted any of this to happen."

"I know, sweetheart." She smiles the best she can at Jack.

"And I'll always be here, Louis, every step of the way. Making sure you keep your word."

"LOUIS!" Sean's gruff voice thunders from outside.

Louis looks at his mother, then at Jack.

"Don't worry, Louis, the living can't see us," his mother says.

A bright light floods the dwelling, and Sean throws open the door. Louis brushes the dirt from his knees as he rises.

"Good, you're dressed, get inside. The police will be here any minute."

He points to the ground. A black tarp covers the body of Doctor Jack Schofield. Alongside that, there's a dead sheepdog. "Bosco attacked your therapist last night, must have thought the doc was going to hurt the sheep. Who knows why animals do the things they do? Had to put her down right there on the spot."

"It's okay, Sean. Tell the police anything you want. I know what happened, and I made a promise never to do it again." Louis walks toward the house, quietly making a vow to himself. "And if it does, I'll take my own life."

CHAPTER 32
ARMING A KILLER

Autumn in Prattsville. A time of golden fields and brilliant-colored trees. Children's thoughts turn to candy and costumes. Flatlanders from the city drive north to pick apples and pumpkins, and to soak in the foliage. The quaint little town would normally be handing out treats, asking for tricks, or getting ready to give thanks, but now, the peaceful village is gripped with fear.

News of last night's haunted baying has spread faster than a blizzard descends in February. The usual traffic in this friendly town is stagnant and people cower behind locked doors. Jenny looks out upon her town from the alcohol-advertised window of her store. *Not one customer all day.*

"Not a single person on the street." She turns to Stacey who's manning the cash register. "You may as well go home, it's almost closing time. Only …" she checks the time on her phone, "two hours left. I think I can handle it from here."

Stacey looks to the door as if the grim reaper is on the other side. "If it's all the same to you, I don't mind staying. Joey didn't come home last night. I left a message for him to call, but so far nothing."

Jenny nods, watching a solitary truck drive down Main Street. The black Land Rover slows and pulls into Young's Hardware Store's parking lot. *Louis.*

She watches him exit the truck and vanish through the doorway.

"Stacey, I'll be right back." She marches out, across the street; a woman on a mission.

Out of the corner of his eye, Louis sees her coming at him and coming fast.

"Okay, Mister. What the hell is going on?"

"Jenny." Louis fumbles with the small package he's purchased. He tosses the small square box wrapped in a brown paper bag through the window onto the passenger seat.

"Don't 'Jenny' me! You have any idea how scared I was last night?"

Curious, Louis asks, "What happened last night?"

"What Happened?" Jenny flails her arms as if Godzilla rose and wiped out half of New York. "You didn't hear that thing last night!"

He shakes his head, bewildered. "What thing?"

"That … that THING! The thing that killed Oren."

"Jenny, you don't believe —"

"LOUIS, I HEARD IT! I was right here, in the middle of Main Street. That thing howled like it had just killed again. It was a victory cry."

"You heard it?"

She throws her arms around Louis. "I thought it was you!"

"Me?" Louis asks sheepishly.

"I thought that thing killed you."

His shoulders drop and he slowly exhales the breath he's been holding. "You shouldn't worry about me, Jenny."

"But I do, Louis, I do."

"Jenny listen." He breaks free of her embrace, "We have to talk, you have to forget about me."

His words hit hard. Her brain tries to process what he's said. She sees his mouth moving; she is certain that he's still talking, but nothing is registering.

"Jenny, I can't stay, I have to leave. I wish there were another way. I wish we could be together, but it's just not possible. I never meant to hurt you." Every cliché, break-up line, and excuse used by every man trying to get out of a relationship seems to blurt out of Louis's mouth.

All Jenny can do is stand there, mouth agape, tears swelling. The determined woman who marched over is reduced to a frail little girl by the words of a man. *Oh, hell no!* She hardens her heart. Fights back the tears and swallows the sickness rising in her gut. "Then go, Louis. Just leave."

"Jenny, I'm—" She closes her eyes, blocking out all images of the Englishman. "Don't, Louis. Just leave."

She hears the truck's door close. The engine starts. The sound of the Land Rover leaving the parking lot fades from her ears, releasing the tears as her heart breaks. Her lips mouth the words, 'I love you, Louis.'

○◑◑◑●◐◐◐○

Pamela Meyers watches the whole scene unfurl through the glass doors of the hardware store. A mother of three girls and a grandmother of five, she has seen her share of breakups and heartaches. What she just witnessed may have been the hardest one yet. As Pamela approaches, all she has to do is open her arms and Jenny melts in. Jenny's sobs soak her sweater as Pamela strokes her air, rocking her slowly and whispering a soothing "shhhhhh."

"I thought he loved me. I thought he cared." She sniffles between breaths. "He didn't even come to town to see me, just came to buy …" She thinks, then asks Pamela, "What did he buy?"

Her soft and comforting voice sounds out of place. "A box of forty-four Magnum shells."

Jenny tears herself from the comfort of Pamela's arms. "Bullets!"

"Yeah. Lots of people are stocking up. That thing has got everyone jumpy."

"He's not jumpy. He's going to kill himself!"

Chapter 33
I Need That Code!

"We have another one, Pete," Vilma Ortiz's voice fills the cruiser.

All morning, Officer Pete Hanlon has been chasing down calls, handling reports ranging anywhere from seeing Bigfoot, mysterious tracks, or foul smells to missing cats, missing farm equipment, and missing people. Among the missing are, Bobby Wilcox, Joey Porter, and Dave Murphy. All three have been missing since yesterday. Vilma has conveyed that Joey was in the station fixing the bathroom, finished, and left around four o'clock.

Pete grabs the mic. "What's this one?"

The radio crackles and then her static voice replies, "Joy Stoltenborg called. Someone dumped an old Dodge pickup at the cable cut entrance on Northwestern and Route 23."

"Check to see if Joey, Bobby, or Dave drives a Dodge truck, please." He asked the question, but already knows the answer. *Dave.*

"One minute." Pete hears the banging of keys. "Dave Murphy drives an '88 Ram pickup. His registration is almost up."

"Northwestern? That's down the road from Kessler's gate." Pete shakes his head. *What did you do, Dave?* "Okay, I'm on it."

He flips the switch, lighting up the top of the cruiser red and blue.

Jenny runs to the tavern, swings open the door. The bright sunlight blinds the late-day drinkers as Jenny yells. "Jimmy, Jimmy Denning! Are you in here?"

A nameless voice calls back, "He's not in here. Close the door."

"Anyone know where he is?"

Another voice in the back yells, "He said he was going into Grand Gorge to fix Andy's security camera at the Tasty Freeze."

Darkness devours the sunlight with a slam of the door. By the time the first beer touches thirsty lips inside, Jenny is halfway to her truck. It takes eight minutes to get to Grand Gorge from Prattsville. Jenny makes it in five. Thirteen calls to Louis's cell phone. All sent to voice mail. *Damn you, Louis.*

The Chevy Blazer skids to a stop in the parking lot of Sundaes Restaurant and Tasty Freeze. Jenny flies from the truck, her eyes fixed like a hawk on Jimmy as he adjusts an external surveillance camera.

"Oh hey, Jenny. What are you doing here?"

"Jimmy, I need the key code to Louis Kessler's front gate." Her voice is stern and militant.

"Jenny I can't give—"

"Jimmy! I don't have time. If you don't give me that code, right now, you'll never buy another bottle of liquor or drink a cold beer in this town again!"

"Which Town? Grand Gorge or Prattsville?" he asks, pulling

out his wallet to check the code, but her glare makes it clear he shouldn't push it.

"Both," she snaps back.

"8211981."

"Thanks."

The Blazer spits gravel until rubber touches asphalt. With a skill matched only by NASCAR drivers, Jenny pushes the twenty-six-year-old engine North on Route 30. Turning right on Route 990V and flying down the long, curved highway, Jenny tries Louis's phone over and over. Still no reply. *Don't do it, Louis.* She takes the hairpin turn onto Flat Creek Road, the Blazer's tires screeching as she turns way too fast. Her front fender kisses the guardrail, sending sparks flying as raspberry paint leaves its mark. *Road's been closed since Irene, and when they finally finished it, it's as narrow and twisty as an intestinal tapeworm!*

It feels like tomorrow by the time Jenny reaches the gate. She punches the code and heads up the dirt road. Turkey hawks gathered in the field barely take notice of the dust cloud rising from the road.

Don't be dead. Don't be dead. Don't be dead, you son of a bitch.

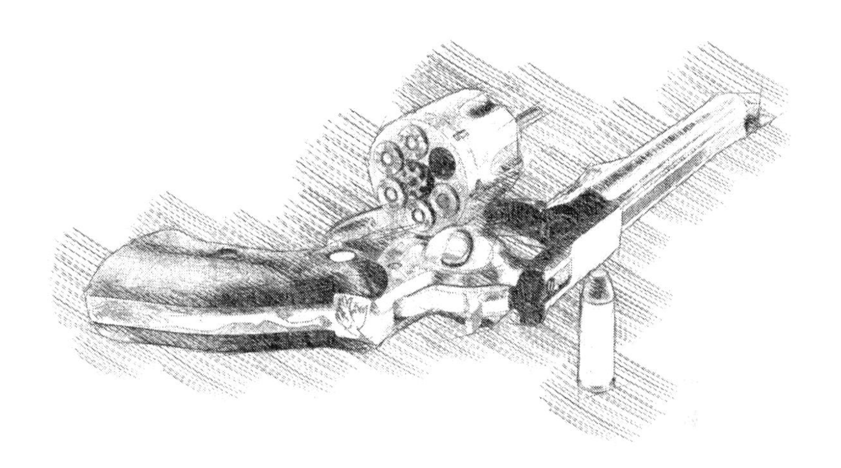

Chapter 34
The Demon Calls

No one can ever claim to know what demons live in the heart and soul of another person. They can only know the demon that lives inside themselves. This particular demon that has tormented Louis Kessler has thrived for far too long. Tonight, Louis means to put an end to his suffering once and for all.

He tosses the brown paper bag onto the kitchen table, hangs up his coat, and grabs the bottle of Cutty Sark. The bottle's opening chills his lips, in contrast to the amber whiskey that warms his body. The bottle stays upright for a long time. Louis prays for the distilled malt grains to quickly absorbs into his bloodstream. He swings the bottle from his lips and gasps for air, then closes his eyes and feels his brain swimming in the sweet nectar of the Speyside region of Scotland.

Louis sits down, composing a letter he's written many times. Only this one is addressed to Jenny, and Officer Pete Hanlon, and the people of Prattsville, asking for forgiveness. He sits back, looking over his final thoughts. Is this what he'll be remembered for? His footsteps are heavy on the oak floor. The forty-four Magnum he retrieves from the bedroom nightstand is heavier.

He stands in the bedroom, feeling the weight of the gun as he positions it in different places against his head.

In the other room, unbeknown to him, the hi-tech security monitor awakens. A flashing green light indicates someone has just entered the key code, killing the power to the electric fence, and is driving through the open cattle gate.

Moments later, the monitor returns to its dormant state, Louis passes it, taking another swig of the whiskey and tossing the pistol on the kitchen table. It hits with a loud thud. Louis empties the contents of the brown paper bag onto the table. The small rectangle box's thud is not as loud. Louis opens the lid and turns the box over. Tiny cylinders slide from the box, scattering as they hit the wood tabletop.

Louis picks up a bullet. Examines it. *Not that big.* He rolls the bullet between his forefinger and thumb. *Shouldn't hurt at all.*

"You hear that, you piece of shit?" He loads the bullet into the chamber. "You don't get to ruin my life anymore. I'm ruining yours!"

He loads another. "This is for the family you robbed from me."

Then another. "This is for my mother."

Again. "This one's for Doctor Schofield."

The fifth one goes in, "This is for Jenny and the happiness you denied her!"

The last bullet. He holds it up. The smooth, cold lead touches his puckered lips. "And this one!" He slams it into the chamber. "This one's for you, Dad! I'll see you in Hell!"

He closes the cylinder, making sure it is nestled securely in place. He places the narrow neck of the whiskey bottle against his lips and tips the bottle upright again. One last drink. *For the road. Better make it a good one.*

He looks at the remaining shells scattered on the table and in the box. "Seems wasteful. Only need one."

His eyelids fall like the final curtain at a Broadway show. His thumb pulls back the hammer. The deadly weapon awaits. His index finger slips in between the finger guard and trigger, the steel is smooth and welcoming. He places the barrel in his mouth. Warm breath fogs the steel as he exhales. In his head, Jim Morrison's voice sings out, *'This is the end. Beautiful friend, the end.'* He greets the darkness with gratifying encouragement. No more lies, no more ghostly visits, no more a slave to celestial lunar cycles. His index finger bends and begins to squeeze the trigger.

Light breaks through the thin curtain of his eyelids, invading the darkness. The sound of a 1995 Chevy Blazer's horn assaults his ears.

Chapter 35
Tiny Whispers

Officer Pete Hanlon turns the cruiser around and heads for the old cable cut on Northwestern off of Route 23. *I swear to God if those three did anything stupid, I'll kill them.*

He picks up the microphone. "Vilma, you there?"

"I'm here, Pete. What's up?"

"You said Joey was in yesterday fixing the bathroom?"

"Yup. Came in a little after lunch and stayed till four." She sounds nonchalant.

Pete's detective skills work to piece the puzzle together. "Was he over by my desk, maybe looking around?"

The electronic voice crackles through the speakers. "He did ask to borrow a pencil and paper. I told him to use one of yours, so I guess, sure, he was looking around. Nothing there but a bunch of old reports and parking tickets."

Pete shakes his head. *Joey, what did you do?*

"You think he swiped a parking ticket?"

"No, I think he got Kessler's security code." Pete presses a little harder upon the accelerator.

"How did he get—"

"It's right there, taped to my monitor, on a Post-It note."

"You think those three got drunk with Kessler and are sleeping it off at his place? I heard he's a bit of a drinker."

"Let's hope that's all it is," Pete says, not holding the microphone's talk button.

"Should I call Kessler and see if he's seen the three?"

"No!" Pete calls into the radio. "No. Wait till I check out the truck. It may be nothing, like everything else this morning." But Pete knows the truck is Dave's. Just like he knows, those three paid Louis a visit last night.

Either the three of them are trying to get their story straight, and rigor mortis set in six hours ago on Mr. Kessler, or I'm gonna have another crime scene on my hands with three more citizens of Prattsville and a missing Englishman. I hope I'm wrong.

Approaching the cable cut, the cruiser rolls up on Northwestern slowly. Sure enough, snuggled between the trees and overgrown shrubs, a 1988 metallic green Dodge Ram pickup truck sits waiting for an owner who will never return.

Shit. "Vilma, can you run a plate?" Pete recites the tags off the beat-up truck.

Almost immediately she responds. "Truck belongs to Dave Murphy."

Fuck, fuck! "Okay thanks. Looks like I'm gonna pay Mr. Kessler a little visit." He throws the mic down and slams his hands against the steering wheel.

A voice, unfamiliar to him, whispers, "*Don't do it.*"
Pete sits up straight as a chill skates down his spine. Tiny hairs on the back of his neck stand at attention. A thought forms and takes

hold. *I don't have to. It's getting late, the sun will be down soon. I can come back in the morning.*

He shakes it off and heads out to interview Louis Kessler.

"Don't do this. Nothing good will come from this," the voice implores.

Pete slows the cruiser. The mountain is gray with twisted, barren, leafless trees. The once rich meadow now lays dying, waiting for winter. Pete ignores the foreboding feeling that grips his spine and pulls the cruiser up to the keypad.

Pressing the intercom he shouts, "Kessler, it's Officer Hanlon, open up." There's no answer. "KESSLER!"

Still no answer.

He picks up the radio mic. "Vilma, read me the number off the post-it note taped to my computer monitor."

"Don't do it," whispers the voice again.

Moments later her voice fills the car. "8-21-1981"

"Don't do it," the voice urges. *"Death awaits you."*

He reaches out to punch in the seven-digit code and stops.

Have you ever had a feeling, as you're about to do something, that reaches deep into your soul and tries to stop you? How many times have you dismissed that tiny voice inside your head that knows better? Perhaps it comes from someone who once walked this earthly plain now sitting beside you and whispering in your ear. How many listen? How many do not?

Pete punches in the code.

Chapter 36
Werewolves Aren't Real!

The Chevy's blaring horn echoing down the mountainside is replaced by Jenny's cries as she shouts Louis's name at the top of her lungs.

Somewhere in his inebriated brain, Louis hears her calls.

He stumbles to the front door, missing the knob and knocking over a lamp. His hands collide with the wall and traverse till they catch the doorknob.

The security monitor wakes once more. "Kessler, it's Officer Hanlon, open up."

Louis shouts back without thinking, "I'm trying, the door is stuck." He flings open the door. His brain tries to process why Officer Hanlon's voice came out of Jenny, who wraps her arms around him.

"Oh, Louis, you're all right."

"Jenny? What are you doing here? You can't be here."

"KESSLER!" the computer's speaker spits out. Moments later, the green indicator light flashes: another intruder has just gained access.

"I was so worried about you." Jenny barges into the cabin, "I tried calling and calling, and when you didn't pick up, I thought the worst."

The forty-four Magnum gleams against the dark wood table top. Bullets are scattered around a lone piece of notepaper.

"Bloody hell, Jenny, You can't be here. You have to leave! Right now." His words running together in one long, slurring mutilation of the English language.

She turns with all the fury of hell. "You were gonna do it! Weren't you?"

"Jshenenny."

"And you're drunk!" She storms over to the table. "What is this? Your little suicide note!" She slams it down on the table. "To think I almost killed myself driving over here."

"You-hav'ta-get-out!" Louis's voice is labored and his breathing is heavy. At first, Jenny thinks he is having a heart attack, and her anger turns to concern.

Beads of sweat cover Louis's face. His soaked shirt clings to his muscles, which appear to be going into spasms.

Outside, the harvest moon climbs over the mountain ridge, ascending into the heavens.

"Louis, are you—"

He pushes past her, swiping the gun from the table. She jumps back. He grabs her arm and thrusts the weapon into her hand. "TAKE IT!" The sudden clarity in his speech bewilders Jenny, "IF YOU HAVE TO, KILL ME! The blood line must be severed!"

"I'm not going to kill—" She stops, feeling the heat from his hands warming her arms even through the winter coat she's wearing, "Louis, you're burning up."

"Listen, Jenny." The strong aroma of whiskey makes it hard for her to concentrate. "My father was attacked by a lycanthrope and survived. Apparently, when someone is attacked and survives, they become a lycanthrope. That's how he contracted this curse. It was in his genes, which he passed on to me. That's why I can never be with you. I'm CURSED!" He looks her in the eyes, holding her tight. "Don't open the door!" His eyes move in an inhuman way. "Stay inside, and don't let me see you!" His voice suddenly drops a couple of octaves. "NO MATTER WHAT!" This last command sounds more like a growl than a drunken Englishman.

His hands tremble. *It's beginning.* He runs to the door. "Lock it! Shut off the lights! And don't look outside!"

Louis disappears into the night. "Remember, the blood line must be severed!"

For a moment, Jenny thinks this is a trick to get her to forgive him. But then a horrible, agonizing scream rattles her very core. Louis sounds as if he is in excruciating pain. She runs to the door, hesitating only a second before throwing it open.

Louis has stumbled off the deck onto the grass by the firepit. The motion detector spotlights illuminate his entire unearthly transformation. Jenny watches in horror as Louis falls to the ground, ripping the clothes from his body. His back arches and falls, twists, and stretches. His hands spread wide and grow. Long claws break from his fingertips, tearing the flesh. Muscles in his arms and legs alter and re-form, creating new ones, attaching to bones, stretching and reorganizing into a creature not meant to walk this earth.

Jenny freezes in absolute horror. Her body instinctively takes over, forcing a deep breath into her lungs. She trembles. Her right hand hits the light switch next to the door. The cabin goes black.

The thing that was once Louis turns. Its face twists in pain. Bones snap and rejoin, fuse back together, and heal. Huge fangs replace human incisors as a long snout stretches, breaking facial bones as it reshapes. His pale flesh disappears as a thick coat of black fur grows from every pore.

Jenny embraces the gun, hugging it close to her chest. The voice of Louis's therapist, unfamiliar to her, pleads, "*lock the door, Jenny.*"

Jenny throws her entire weight against the door, finding the deadbolt and securing it tight.

"*Good girl, Jenny. Now don't make a sound.*"

Unspeakable horrors are transpiring only yards away, and the only thing stopping the beast from killing her is a wooden door no thicker than a matchbook. The sounds of pain subside, and a low growl takes their place.

Jenny slows her breathing and tries to suppress the throbbing of her beating heart. A bolt of lightning flashes, throwing rays of light onto the floor, and Jenny yelps. She clasps her hand over her mouth. It's too late. The beast senses prey is near. A low roll of thunder proclaims death is on its way.

A board creaks on the steps leading up to the deck. The beast is coming closer. Heavy footsteps fall upon the planks of wood. Jenny stops breathing. She feels the cold steel of the gun and thinks of pulling the hammer back, getting ready for the attack. From what she remembers, there are two clicks. The first secures the barrel in position: the second locks the hammer in place. Both sounds will surely provoke an attack. She chooses to remain silent. Air passing through her nose reverberates in her ears, sounding a thousand times louder than it actually is. She drops her jaw, trying to expand her windpipe to silence the noise.

Another flash of lightning, but this time she doesn't make a sound. A mirror on the back wall catches the movement outside. Across the room, reflected in the mirror, two burning yellow-green eyes peer into the cabin. The only move Jenny makes is to slowly close her eyes. The last thing she sees are razor-sharp, white fangs emerging from beneath a dark snout. *Please God, please ... please.*

From a distance, a single gunshot rings out. The beast snarls. Steam fogs the window. Turkey hawks fly overhead. The beast takes two leaps and clears the deck, landing with a thud on the cold ground. Jenny gasps like a drowning victim coming up for air. She spins, cocking the gun and aiming it at the door. She backs up gingerly, fanning the gun barrel at every window in the small cabin. Her leg hits the table. Bullets roll and drop to the floor. Her eyes move from word to word on the note Louis wrote.

"My fault ... I killed Oren Goodman ... I killed Bobby, Joey, and Dave ..." Her hand covers her mouth. Overwhelming sorrow mixes with pure terror. She continues reading. *"Couldn't help myself ... tell Jenny I love her and I'm sorry."*

Streams of tears run down Jenny's face, blurring her vision, stopping her from reading further. She frantically scans the room for a phone. *Why doesn't he have a phone?* Then she realizes her own cell phone is in her back pocket.

"Prattsville Sheriff Department. How can we help?"

"Louis Kessler. It was Louis Kessler. He killed all those people," Jenny whispers.

"Miss, can you speak up? It sounded like you said—"

"Yessssss, That's exactly what I said, Louis Kessler is the killer. And no, I can't speak up because he could be right outside. I'm at Kessler's place. Get Pete Hanlon over here now!"

"He's out of the office on another call, but I'll let him know ..."

'Are you out of your fucking mind?' is what Jenny wants to say. Instead, Vilma's voice cuts off as Jenny hangs up.

Her mind races with scenarios. *Get to the truck. Get out of here. What if that thing is out there waiting? Stay in here, and what? Wait for it to break in? That didn't really work too well for Oren Goodman.*

She backs into a corner. *Does it know I'm here? IT! Jesus, that IT is Louis!* Her puffy winter coat flattens against the back wall. Her legs weaken and she slides down, keeping the gun trained on the door. A streak of light races across the sky followed by a thunderous crack. Jenny jumps.

What the hell is happening? Werewolves aren't real!

Chapter 37
Pete's Discovery

The metal cattle gate swings open and Pete coaxes the cruiser through. Swirling storm clouds circle in the twilight, scattering patches of gray against the blue canvas of the nighttime sky. A storm brewing over Syracuse heads toward Albany. Pete drives up the dirt road. Between the shrubs and trees off to the left, he spots a small hog tied to a sapling. He slows the cruiser and shines the car's spotlight into the field. The hog's eyes shine red when the beam hits just right. Hanlon grabs a flashlight and his shotgun and heads out into the meadow. He slides the stock back on the shotgun, loading the chamber. A frightened pheasant jumps and alerts several more, who take to the air. Pete takes two short fast breaths. If this was hunting season and Pete knew how to cook, he might be enjoying a nice pheasant under glass later tonight. But fate has darker plans for Officer Hanlon. He wipes the sweat from his face before continuing. This time, the gun stock nests snug under his cheek. A vein in his neck throbs, pushing against the stock, making it hard to focus the barrel.

The ground is soft and spongy, layers of thatch cushioning his steps. A westerly wind races through the woods and creates currents in the grass. Like an invisible sailing vessel gliding over the Atlantic, the wind moves the hay in a turbulent sea. There's a winter smell from the north chilling the air, staking its claim upon the Catskills for the upcoming months. The full moon crests over the mountain range.

A committee of turkey hawks peppers the sky. Some descend to nearby trees, while the braver ones, or perhaps those more selfish, hungrier, merely hop back and take a more strategic line of sight.

Pete disregards the hog and moves on to see what has attracted such a large gathering of scavengers. Even though the woods have grown dark, the setting sun's ambient glow still provides enough light to make out some kind of remains dispersed throughout the field. Trampled down grass from the hawks fighting over scraps can be seen in three distinct areas. One, twenty yards away, is out in the open, while the other two are closer to a rock wall. Pete draws closer and shines the powerful beam of the flashlight to get a better look. Turkey hawks perched in the trees protest in a chorus of screeches. Pete stops and surveys the area. Small ribbons of ripped denim jeans and dark blood-stained fabric hang like tinsel from nearby hay stalks and shrubbery. Sensing the puzzle coming together, he moves light beam from one horrifying area to the next. His mouth drops open when he sees the red baseball cap. "Make America—" are the only words legible in the blood-soaked, torn hat. He forces his throat to close off, not allowing the diner's pot roast special he enjoyed earlier access to the outside world.

Moving in a wide berth so as not to trample any evidence, he proceeds to the next clearing. Moving even more cautiously now, he comes upon the remains of Joey Porter. His Humphrey

Bogart teeth still push past his upper lip, but beyond that, not much remains. His neck has been torn out, and from what Pete can see, most of his chest cavity is missing.

Pete shoulders the shotgun, placing the flashlight parallel to its barrel. He scans the forest, stopping at every suspicious tree and rock that looks like it might attack. The light hits a large oak tree and Pete almost fires. The body of Bobby Wilcox lies slumped against the rock wall. With outstretched wings, a turkey hawk there defends its meal, letting out a fierce screech before struggling with a stubborn vein in Bobby's stump of a neck. Pete contorts his face in disgust. A deafening crack erupts from the barrel, scaring the reluctant hawks into the night air.

In the back of his head, he keeps telling himself that the killer is long gone, but if it could take out Dave and the boys, he isn't going to take any chances.

Pete reaches for the microphone clipped to his shoulder, his thumb shaking over the button. He goes to speak but only coughs, his mouth too dry to form words. His tongue searches for moisture.

Finally, he says, "Vilma, you better send backup to the Kessler place. I found Bobby, Dave, and Joey." His thumb slides from the button. "Or what's left of them," he murmurs.

Vilma's voice cuts through the cold dark air. "Did they beat up that English fella? Should I call Dave's wife to come and bail him out?"

"Vilma! They're dead! Bobby, Joey, Dave … they're all dead!"

"Is Kessler dead? Did Kessler do it?"

A bolt of lightning streaks across the sky, followed by a low, rolling rumbling. The ever-growing dark sky fills with thunderclouds as the storm descends upon Prattsville. Officer Hanlon goes to the cruiser, wind pushing upon his back. He clicks down the button of the mic. "I don't know, but I'm gonna find out. I hope not … If he did, he's one sick son of a bitch."

Chapter 38
The Blood Line Must Be Severed

Jenny sits huddled in the corner of the cabin, knees pulled in tight against her chest. The heavy metal revolver is aimed at the door. Her arms burn from its weight. Light tapping sounds break the silence. Jenny swings the gun left, then right. The sound is coming from all around the cabin. Her brain scrambles until she realizes she's hearing raindrops falling on the tin roof. She lowers the gun and sighs. But moments later, red and blue lights flood the cabin through the windows, and Jenny screams and aims the gun toward the kitchen window, where the light is the brightest.

A loud voice, muffled by the walls and rain, suddenly reverberates in the small dwelling. "Kessler! It's Officer Hanlon! Come out with your hands up!"

It takes a moment for Jenny to register that it's Pete outside using the PA system in his squad car, calling for Louis to surrender.

"KESSLER!"

She gets to her feet, not sure what to do. She sees Hanlon block out the flashing lights through the kitchen window as he makes his way to the front door.

"Pete!" She runs to the heavy wooden door. Unlocking the deadbolt, she swings the door open. "Pete! Pete, it's me, Jenny!"

Hanlon, gun trained on the door, quickly pulls the gun up in a resting ready stance. "Jenny? Where's Kessler?" He grabs her arm to pull her from the cabin.

Jenny screams and darts back into the house. "Pete, get in here!"

For a split-second, Pete is perplexed, then spins and drops the gun to a firing stance, scanning the deck and beyond that, the field. Thunder crashes and a flash of light allows Pete to get a glimpse of the empty field.

"PETE, GET IN HERE!"

Hanlon backs into the cabin, checking his flanks. He moves around the cabin, looking for Louis. Jenny throws herself against the door, locking it with fury.

"Where is he? Where's Kessler?" Pete kicks the bathroom door open, fanning the gun inside.

"He's out there!" she screams, pointing toward the front door with the hand holding the gun. A shine catches Pete's eye and his brain registers *GUN.*

He takes the aggressive stance he's been trained to assume. "Jenny, drop the gun."

"You don't understand," she cries.

But he yells at her anyway. "Jenny, Kessler killed Dave, Bobby, and Joey. He probably killed Oren too! I need you to drop the gun!"

Jenny yells back, "It wasn't him! I mean, it isn't him. Pete, Louis is a were—"

A thunderclap shakes the cabin. Lightning strikes a tree at the edge of the field. The storm is right on top of the small house.

A tremendous, unnatural howl replaces the crack of thunder, drowning out the anger of the storm. The creature is close.

Jenny screams as Pete rushes to the door.

"Don't open it! He'll kill us!" Jenny shouts as she retreats to her corner. She does her best to aim at the door, but she's shaking terribly, like a heroin addict trying to get clean.

"What the hell is that?" Pete turns to Jenny.

Her lips quiver. Her eyes well with tears. She lowers the shaking gun. Softly, barely audibly, not loud enough for a mouse to hear, she tells him, "That's Louis."

The rain pelts down hard. Water cascades off the roof in sheets. Outside, a predator searches for an opening. Inside, its prey is trapped. It's a terrible thing to live in fear, knowing that death is right outside your door, stalking you. Tonight, for the first time, Jenny and Pete are part of the food chain.

A heavy thud lands on the deck. The cruiser's blue and red lights are once again blocked out, this time by the shape of a much larger, hairy figure.

Jenny fires; the smell of gunpowder fills the cabin. The window frame shatters.

"Jenny!" Pete yells. "I want this son-of-a-bitch alive."

"It ain't Louis!" Jenny shouts back.

Heavy thumps are heard as the beast paces the deck on all fours, growling as it exhales.

Jenny presses her back against the wall, tracking the movement with the barrel of her gun. Lightning throws windowpane silhouettes on the floor and thunder shakes the cottage. Another flash of lightning reveals dark fur matted down from the rain, blocking one of the windows. The snarling face of a wolf like creature, bearing its ivory fangs, paralyzes Jenny with fear.

Pete spins and takes aim. He squeezes the trigger and the bullet shatters the window. Wind rushes in, sending the curtains flapping as tempestuous rain pours through the broken glass.

The creature's snarls are loud, even over the pouring rain. Pete takes a step backward, closer to Jenny, and stops. His eyes focus on the broken window. The image of Oren Goodman's shattered window invades his thoughts. He knows at any moment this battle is going to be resolved, one way or another.

He takes another step. Breaking glass, howling winds, thunderous rain, and a snarling beast crashes into their world.

But the sound of the breaking window does not come from the shattered one at the front of the house, as Pete expected. It comes from the bedroom. Pete spins, firing three shots blindly into the dark room. Each time the muzzle flashes, it lights the blackness — a strobe effect, freeze-framing the muscular beast preparing to pounce. Before he can pull the trigger a fourth time, powerful hindquarters launch the massive figure forward, knocking Pete to the floor. He fires two more rounds, hitting the creature in the torso before its teeth are upon him.

Screams of agony fill the cabin as razor-sharp fangs tear deep into his flesh. Claws scratch at anything they come in contact with, shredding tile, wood, and flesh.

Then, over the screams and snarls, one sharp, ear-splitting crack rings out, and the creature falls dead.

Pete sees Jenny standing there, her arms still outstretched behind where the creature stood. A thin whisper of smoke snakes up to the rafters from the barrel of the forty-four.

Claws reshape as fingers, razor incisors return to human teeth, thick fur retreats into soft flesh. Jenny watches as the savage beast that has terrorized the town of Prattsville turns back into Louis Kessler, the man she loved.

Pete grabs at his open wounds. “Help me, Jenny! Help me stop the bleeding.”

His breathing is heavy, but his wounds are not life-threatening. If they can stop the bleeding, he will survive.

“Help me, Jenny! Help me, please!”

She stares down at Louis’s naked body. *So much pain, so much conflict his whole life.* She thinks back on what Louis told her, ‘when someone is attacked and survives, they become a lycanthrope—a werewolf.’ She then remembers the last words he spoke to her, ‘The bloodline must be severed.’ Her eyes turn sorrowful. She looks at Pete. He begs one last time. The glimmer of hope on his face is replaced with shock as she raises the gun and whispers, “I’m sorry.”

A tiny movement of her finger releases the bullet, killing Officer Peter Hanlon.

In a quaint hunting cabin in the woods of Prattsville, two bodies lie dead: one of the man she loved, and one of the man who loved her.

She drops the gun. It lands by Louis’s hand.

Police sirens rise out in the rain as several cruisers pull into the driveway.

Chapter 39
All Questions Answered

3 a.m. The small cabin is swarming with officers inside and out. All the photographs have been taken, the evidence all collected, and Jenny's statement has been recorded. She sits with a police trauma blanket wrapped around her to prevent shock, as if what she's witnessed could ever be erased by a stiff wool blanket. One by one, the two black body bags are lifted onto ambulance gurneys and removed from the scene.

A boyish-faced officer looks over her statement. "Is there anything else you want to add?"

In Jenny's version of what happened, she recounts when she got to the cabin, because she feared Louis was about to commit suicide. *This part is true.* He became violent because of the amount of alcohol he'd consumed. *Somewhat true.* When Officer Hanlon arrived, Louis attacked them, they struggled, both had a gun, but Hanlon fired two shots into Louis, *also true,* before Louis fired the fatal shot that killed Officer Hanlon. *Not true.* Louis put the gun on the table for some reason, and when he did, I shot him. *The last part was true.*

She gives this version because no one would believe the truth.

The last question the baby-faced officer asks is, “Why was Mr. Kessler naked?”

Jenny’s answer would later be corroborated by Jimmy Dennings. “He would always get naked when he drank.”

All the forensic results match Jenny’s story and confirm three gunshot wounds were the cause of death. The bullet that killed Officer Hanlon came from Louis Kessler’s gun. With the confession in the suicide note and the bodies found by Officer Hanlon, the evidence against Kessler is indisputable. The motive is still in question, but who knows why serial killers do what they do?

Since Louis Kessler’s death is not labeled a suicide, Louis’s estate passes to Jenny, as stated in his will. She’d known Louis had an air of wealth about him, but it is more money than Jenny has ever imagined. She sells the store and moves away. Some people say she traveled to Europe. Others say she moved into Louis’s apartment in New York City. Although those who knew her might say you could never take the country out of a girl like Jenny, Most of the residents of Prattsville like to think she is living on a farm, raising sheep and perhaps a family as well.

As for the town of Prattsville, it’s still a quaint little town where neighbors say hello and talk on the front porch. Townwide garage sales and Autumn festivals come and go. Mud-covered, rusted pickups still fill the parking lots and people have a real sense of American pride. The only crime is an occasional parking ticket or a late-night sobriety infraction, but other than that it’s a peaceful place where people feel comfortable leaving their doors unlocked at night.

However, if you ask the residents of Prattsville, even to this day, a sense of fear grips this small upstate town whenever the moon grows full and the winter winds blow down from the North. The five-pointed star still adorns the wall of the tavern and both candles burn bright every twenty-eight days. The town fears that the ghastly howl may someday be heard again. One thing is for certain: no one will ever forget the terror that followed when an Englishman came to Prattsville.

Epilogue

Seven Months Later

Welcome Home, Miss Kessler?

Jenny drives a small, used Fiat she purchased in London for the drive up north. After all, if she's planning on making this new country her home, she might as well have a dependable car. It's taken a little getting used to driving on the other side of the road, but once she got out of the city and into the country, things got easier. And where she's going, not many people travel.

There is a mist in the air, making everything look gray. The sky is gray, the air is gray, even the dried grass, normally a golden wheat color, has taken on a drab olive-green hue. An endless wall of gray shades rise from this valley, traveling up the mountainside and touching the sky. The landscape of this new country looks like a turbulent sea, with high cresting waves and deep troughs frozen in place and now covered by flowing blades of grass. On the uncommon days when the sun does appear, it will turn this medieval countryside into a fairytale landscape straight out of

King Arthur and the Knights of the Round Table. She follows her phone's GPS, not sure if she can trust the electronic voice, until she comes to a small signpost at a fork in the road. Her satellite navigator's accuracy is confirmed when she slows and reads the name printed on the post.

Five more miles, she thinks, looking at the paper on the passenger side seat. Meeting Mr. Landis, Realtor at Builth Wells House. Bear left at fork off of A470 onto LD2 3PJ in the town of Erwood. She remembers hearing his voice on the phone. *It will look like someone's private road, but trust me, that's the route leading into town. Just keep driving. It's narrow, so don't go too fast. You never know who's coming around the corner. I'll be in the yellow building toward the left when you come into town. You can't miss it; there'll be a red phone box directly before you and an old stone church beyond that.* With his strong accent, Jenny had hardly been able to make out what he was saying, but she found it refreshing and sweet, and she's reminded of a man she once loved. But Jenny also smirks and thinks, *who names their streets LD2 and 3PJ? Sounds like some droids out of a movie.*

"Narrow" is not the word for it. If left untraveled for more than a week, the hedges and brushes on both sides seem as if they could close up the passage and no one would ever know this place existed. But for Jenny, it will soon be home. *And I thought Route 30 back home was narrow.*

Jenny coasts down the winding road that leads into town, stopping only to let a herd of mud-covered sheep move from the road. As she pulls into the town, she re-checks the paper for which building she is supposed to meet the Realtor to finalize the transaction.

She parks the car and walks to the town pub. *That's ironic,* she thinks, looking at the sign hanging above the door. *If the lamb was slaughtered, why is it a wolf's head on a pike?*

As Jenny walks through the door she gasps, clasping her hand over her mouth. A typical English pub. Nothing special, but for a girl who had previously traveled no farther than Albany, every experience is a new one. But this one offers something unique. It's not the customers sitting around talking or reading the paper or playing darts. It's the blood-red pentagram painted on the back wall. There are two unlit candles on each side.

"Oh, don't mind that, deary, haven't needed that for years," the barmaid shouts out from behind the long wooden bar. "Can I help you?"

Her accent's thick, but Jenny makes it out. "I'm looking for Mr. Landis."

A tall, elderly man steps forward. He's a handsome gent, sporting round glasses, and gray beard sprinkled with traces of his youth throughout, "I'm Mr. Landis. You must be Jenny, from America? We spoke on the mobile."

Mobile? "Oh, the cell phone, I have to get used to a whole new way of speaking," she chuckles. "You know, you have the same name as a Hollywood—"

"Yes, I'm quite aware. Been told many times." He gestures to a table and removes some papers from his briefcase. "Are you sure you don't want to look at the place before you buy it?"

Jenny nods. "I have a pretty good idea of what I'm buying. Your website's photos were very detailed." She doesn't want to tell him she had a firsthand account of the property from her discussions with Louis, the previous owner.

"I have to tell you, people think the place is cursed. Been on the market for years, but no one wants it."

"Oh, why is that?"

"On account of the murders," a mean-faced fellow playing darts calls out.

"Murders?" Jenny turns and addresses the man.

"Yeah, two of 'em. A woman and a doctor. Not at the same time, but both of them were torn apart."

"All right!" John yells at the man. "There'll be no more talk about that." He turns to Jenny and in a softer voice says, "They were both terrible accidents involving animals. A mad dog, I believe one of them was."

"I'm sure nothing like that will happen now," Jenny says, picking up the pen and signing the deed. "I hope not."

She cradles her belly. The instinct for a mother to protect her young is one of the strongest forces on Earth. Her seven-month bump announces to everyone her present condition. "Besides, the baby's father is from here and wanted to raise the child in the place where it all began."

The barmaid sets down a pint. "I'll bring you over a nice cup of tea, dear. You'll love it here. It's a great place to raise a family. Will the father be joining you anytime soon?" she asks.

A smile fades from Jenny's face, "Sadly, no. He died."

"I'm sorry, Miss …" she pauses. "I'm sorry I didn't get your last name."

"It's Louvel. Jenny Louvel, but my baby will have his father's last name. Kessler."

A stray dart hits the wall, missing the target completely.

"I've only missed that board once before," the mean-faced fella mutters.

Jenny turns. "Do you know a lot about this town, Mr. Landis?"

He smiles. "You may say the town wouldn't exist if it weren't for me."

He walks Jenny outside and gives her directions to her new home. She shakes his hand and thanks him for everything he has done.

"Welcome to East Proctor."

The End

Acknowledgments

To my parents, Jack and Carole MacKnight, I can never thank you enough for your continuing love. You have always encouraged me to chase my dreams and stood behind whatever I wanted to do in life. I am so grateful and thankful to be surrounded by so many wonderful friends and family members who supported and encouraged me through every step of the creative process. Everyone has been tremendously helpful, and I wish to thank you all.

I would like to thank the people of Prattsville and all the places I mentioned. Everyone is extremely nice and welcoming. This is real America, and I feel I have not captured the true beauty of this town. I hold a special place for Prattsville in my heart. As a teenager, it was a place where my dad and I would stop at the diner and have breakfast before going hunting. As I got older, it became a haven for my seclusion. It's always been a trusted spot to buy groceries, whiskey, and when much-needed repairs on the cabin required attention, Young's Hardware always seemed to have just the right part to fix it. It's a town where everyone is friendly, the apple pies are always warm, and the beers are always cold. *My kind of place.*

Next, I want to thank Director John Landis, not only for allowing me to use his name along with the name of the town of East Proctor, but for creating the ultimate werewolf movie, *An American Werewolf in London (1981)*—the true standard all other werewolf movies will forever have to live up to—not to mention the film that scared a 17-year-old Gary MacKnight as he sat in a dark theater watching David Naughton transform into a werewolf with the help of Oscar-winning effects by Rick Baker.

As I told John Landis, I didn't start out by using his movie, *American Werewolf in London*, to write this book. But things just fell into place. I counted over twenty references to his movie, but I'm sure there are more. True fans might be able to get all of them. Let me know how many you found (LeaveaMark4me@gmail.com); one was even a surprise to me! I hope it had the *ah-ha* effect I hoped to achieve on the last page, which tied all the other references into place.

I'd like to thank Christine for listening to all my crazy rants. One of them sparked the idea for this book. Many were just the ranting of a lunatic. (from the Latin *lunaticus,* meaning *an extremely foolish or eccentric person—specifically* the belief that the *moon* causes intermittent insanity). I thought it fitting.

I'd like to thank all my friends for their encouragement and constant support throughout these past months as I dribbled on about *'my book'*. I was also really touched when I offered ARCs (Advanced Reader Copies), where people read your book before its release and suggest feedback. I received an overwhelming amount of love and support. Friends I haven't heard from in years reached out to me and were there for me. I thank you!

There is someone I have to say a special thanks to: Laura Williams. *In fact, the character of Officer Hanlon was originally named Officer Pete Williams for her, until I learned the constable for the town of Prattsville was a man named Officer Steve Williams. I thought people would think I based the character on him (which I wouldn't mind except that I killed him at the end of the book, and I didn't want to get parking tickets every time I went to town).*

Laura is one of those people I got very excited for to read the first draft of my manuscript. To watch her read my book was to see every word expressed on her face. She laughed at the funny parts, she grew sad at the tragic parts, and smiled when the words were arranged just right. Getting lost in the pages of a book is what every author hopes they can do for a reader. To draw the reader in and make them see *our world* through *our words* as if they were there is truly transpiring. I also want to thank her husband, Rande. He's the first one who had to sift through my chicken scratch and make corrections. He did a lot of cleaning up of my first draft (and believe me, there was lot of cleaning to do), just so I didn't look completely illiterate when I asked other people to read it.

Speaking of the other people I forced to read the rough drafts and give me input, I'd like to thank each of them for making this a better book. Thank you, Vilma, for catching all the little mistakes, Natasha, for picking out small details I overlooked, and Sean for catching the big ones. Sean is a fountain of countless grammatical answers, and he polished the final draft to make it shine like a diamond.

Last but never least, I'd like to thank Lynn Canon, who edited the book. If you think you write well, just give your manuscript to an editor and wait. She did an amazing job, and I can't thank her enough.

Thank you all for reading my book. I hope you enjoyed it! I'd love to hear from you, so please email me at LeaveaMark4me@gmail.com and let me know what you thought.

If you liked this book, please go to Amazon and add a review (but please, no spoilers).

If you enjoyed this book, you're going to love *LEAVE a MARK.*

Soon to be Released

Please enjoy the first chapter...

"Find a mark. Leave a mark. It is time."
A quiet voice whispers in the darkness,
calling forth an ancient memory.

Chapter 1
New York City
Present Day

IN AN UPPER EAST SIDE APARTMENT, JONATHAN TAYLOR, A 55-YEAR-OLD architect, scrambles to his feet, lost and confused; he moves around the apartment he has called home for more than 20 years as though he's never seen it before.

"Cassandra! We have to go!" His loud, booming voice breaks the silence as he stumbles about the room designated as his office. Cassandra appears in the doorway. It's quite unusual for his 22-year-old cat-like daughter to be up so early, but wiping the sleep from her eyes, she witnesses a most unusual sight: her father ransacking the otherwise well-kept room, tossing papers and books as he frantically moves from bookcase to bookcase.

"Dad, what's going on?"

The morning sun is just breaking through the blinds, but already the city is alive and active. Steam escapes from steel plates lying on the black asphalt as the early morning fare jockeys cut through the rising mist, racing towards Penn Station.

"Cazz, where are my books? The photo albums? From Africa —"

"Dad, you don't have to be at work for another two hours, and I don't have class today, so I'm going back to bed," she says turning to walk down the hall.

"I'm not going to work today," he shouts as she enters her bedroom. "Or any other day for that matter."

He speaks more softly, hoping she doesn't hear him, but not softly enough for her young ears. "What do you mean you're not—"

"Remember? Remember when I was in Italy with your mother, remember, I kept telling her I felt like I'd been there before? Do you remember me telling you that? I wonder if she would remember?"

"I think I remember," Cassandra says, scratching her head. Her long brunette hair, the color of milk chocolate toffee, is as disheveled as a squirrel's nest reflects how Cassandra is thinking. "What do you mean you're not—"

"Do you think she'll remember if I call her?"

CALL MOM? The mere suggestion stops her cold, and like a stinging slap across the face, dislodges any remnant of slumber.

"I think it was Florence? And then again in Scotland! And then, oh, when we took that trip to Australia last year. Do you remember, I felt it again?" her father rambles.

"I don't think calling Mom is a good idea. She's still not speaking to you. Not since the divorce."

Christ, it's been 10 years, Jonathan realizes.

But before Cassandra can say another word, her father's thoughts race to another topic.

"I have to call my lawyer and then make arrangements with the bank. I have to call them too. No, I'll go down there. Where are my keys?"

"Uh, Dad, I'll be right back," Cassandra says, slipping down the hall, unnoticed by her father. She picks up her cell phone, and with a frantic few swipes and clicks, calls her brother.

On the other end, a sleepy, disorientated voice answers the phone. "Cazz?"

"Trevor! Oh, thank God you're up!"

"Cazz, do you know what time it is?" His voice borders on confused and annoyed.

"It's early. I know—" Cassandra begins, only to be cut off abruptly.

"EARLY? It's not EARLY in Arizona! It's the middle of the FUCKING night! And NO, I wasn't up. You woke me. But I have to be up in three hours, so this better be good." Now fully awake, his confusion fades and only annoyance prevails.

"Trev, listen! It's Dad, something is wrong," she pleads into the phone. "He's acting really weird."

"Weird how? Weird like he had a stroke, or weird like he's walking around the city with no clothes on?"

"He's talking about leaving! And not like when he left Mom. He's talking about leaving the city!"

"The city?" Trevor asks, now completely bewildered.

"Yes! And," she pauses, listening to her father bang around "Trevor, he said he's not going into work!"

This captures Trevor's full attention. As far back as he could remember, his father never missed a day of work. He built his practice by himself, acquiring one company after another until his firm was the leader in the architectural world. "Put him on the phone."

"Dad, it's Trevor. He wants to talk to you," she says handing her father the phone.

"TREVOR! Oh, I'm so glad you called," unaware it was Cassandra who initiated the call.

"Dad?" Trevor's voice proceeds with caution as slowly as a springtime bather enters a mountain stream. "Hey, what's going on?"

"I'm going on a trip. Well, more like a journey, a trek. Sort of a voyage of, um, discovery, and I want you to come. You and your sister. You *have* to come."

"Dad, I have work. I can't just pick up and go. Wait, where are you going? What are you talking about? Dad, what is going on?" The questions tumble from his mouth faster than his brain can think of them.

"I need to leave—"

"Leave where?"

"I have someplace I need to be—"

"Like where?"

Jonathan fumbles for the right words, cautious not to scare Trevor, or worse, trigger something that would prevent him from leaving. "All I know is, I want you and your sister with me. To make sense of everything."

"Make sense of what?"

"Son, I *need* you to come with me."

The commanding tone reminds Trevor of the times, as a child, when his father taught him a valuable life lesson. It wasn't a demanding voice, but a powerful *now listen to me* voice that made Trevor stop and contemplate the events that were about to unfold.

There was a long pause, and before Trevor could say anything else, Jonathan's voice grew suddenly calm, and he whispered softly, "Trevor, I'm dying."

Made in the USA
Columbia, SC
21 August 2021

44115127R00129